The blind squirrel & other Arizona animal tails

*By Jack Grenard
& 14 other
Arizona authors*

Carefree Communications

Copyright © 1995 by Jack Grenard

All rights reserved under International and Pan-American Copyright Conventions. Published in the United States of America by Carefree Communications, Inc. No part of this book may be used or reproduced in any manner whatsoever without written permission except for brief quotations embodied in critical articles and reviews. For information, address Carefree Communications, Inc., Box 5268, Carefree, Arizona 85377; call 602.488.1462, fax -5376, email jgren12345@aol.com. 1995 price, US$14.95.

First edition

Grenard, Jack, et al
The blind squirrel & other Arizona animal tails/by Jack Grenard et al
p.cm.
ISBN 0-9631487-1-0
1. Nature. I. Title.

Manufactured in the United States of America
9 8 7 6 5 4 3 2 1
First Edition

Cover
Pat Lyon of Tucson created the marvelous montage; devious Jack added the dark glasses.

Contents

    1 Two wrens in an outhouse
  21 Battle with cattle
  37 Coyote voice
  45 Shaggy dogs and real
  59 My horse healed me
  73 Packrat chronicles
  93 Snakes alive
115 More stories from other authors
145 Other animals, other stories
183 That blind squirrel

The blind squirrel & other Arizona animal tales

Preface

Animals: Maybe the closest we get to spirits

It occurs to me, upon embarking on the project of publishing Arizona animal stories, that this book could help open our eyes to the subtle world around us. The lives that other species live, with some exceptions, go on almost on another plane, nearly invisible to us. Yes, the other species coexist with us but we know so little about them that they could as well belong to a parallel universe, rarely visible within our narrow spectrum of sensations.

    Yet these other species communicate with each other, soar, burrow, metamorphose, live, and die, all usually outside of our sphere of knowledge or at least of our interest.

    "Towhee?" a young woman asks. "What's that?" Why would she have heard of or seen or whistled at a dull gray-brown bird the size of a cactus wren? Yet the species is common in my part of Arizona.

    Who except the careful observer or the student of Nature has seen packrats running in daytime under the protection of ground cover between busy Hayden Road in Scottsdale and a crowded parking lot at Price-CostCo? These creatures live with us and around us. We find coyote scat, hear coyote songs in the night and maybe a great horned owl hooting, but mostly the other species go their own ways, interacting with us as little as possible.

Perhaps we who have lived closer to them than city dwellers who see only the works of man will open some eyes and some hearts with this book. That is the hope of all of these authors.

Unless otherwise credited, these stories and essays are my work. Some first appeared in the local weekly, the *Foothills Sentinel.*

—Jack Grenard
Carefree, Arizona
25 October 1995

Dedication

To my parents, Edward Merrill Grenard and Jane Ashmore Grenard, who introduced me to the magic of the non-human world at an early age in Galesburg, Illinois. And to Geoffrey Platts, who, through his own observations and essays, brought me back in touch with a world I left ages ago and thought I'd lost. (He also provided two stories for this book and caught my editing misses.) And to my first and last wife, Jane Elizabeth Grenard, who enhances my appreciation of the animals. And to our children, Mark and Lizz, who appear in this book because they lived it.

A tale of two wrens in an outhouse
By Geoffrey Platts

*T*he limpid, descending call of the canyon wren reminds me of my two (soon to be seven) outhouse guests. In late May [1994] a pair of canyon wrens chose Platts's privy in which to propagate. I was pleased about this, but you can imagine there were some logistical problems. Like the wrens, I too had to answer the call of Nature, a morning man, in fact. Not wishing to incommode the sitting wren, I gave serious thought to going wild for a while. Having backpacked a lot, I had ample practice in bush squatting and found it quite a salutary procedure. And there certainly wasn't a lack of space with my backyard of 2.9 million acres. I should add that, tho' my backyard is public (that is, federal lands), it is quite private.

No, thought I, it's one thing to be obliging and hospitable to our feathered friends but it's altogether another thing to be driven from one's own precious privy.

What to do? I simply couldn't fling open the door, barge in—all six feet menacingly filling the frame—and bombastically bash away with my b.m. That would terrify the bird and she'd be hard put to even fly out, given the narrow door.

I went wild for a few days. Such is the price of reverence for life. Then I came up with a compromise. I would leave the G. john (G. for *Geoffrey*) door a third open, and when my b.m. visitation was at hand I would steal up on the door and very slowly open it. The wren, I figured, would respond to the movement—not my impending movement, but that of the door—and split. It worked.

With this warning, the bird had time to make a dignified exit. And so she did. I then took up position for the diurnal duty and got on with the job, reflecting smugly, as I always do, on the five gallons of water I was saving with my non-flush earth (and earthen) latrine.

Little wren was back in a trice, hopping from rock to rock, quite close, seemingly indignant and irked. At one point she hopped inside the privy within inches of my very still feet. She wanted me out—and pronto. I know better than to argue with a woman. I left, but reluctantly. She was giving me just enough time for the essential, but not a minute more to think noble thoughts, to perhaps ponder the imponderable. I would have to vacate the throne, to go sit on a chair or something equally mundane.

So that was the ritual of compromise Mrs. Wren and I had set up. Then one day a bit of a miracle happened. For years I had been imitating the canyon wren's descant call, and would often answer if I heard it. I had a splendid idea (not while sitting on the john, alas). Why not try to call the bird out instead of always going through the door routine?

Both the local female and the male (who, you'll be glad to hear, ladies, helps out with the nest-building and the feeding of the young) had to know my feeble mimicking of their song. The question was, Would she-on-the-nest respond and react to me? I want you to know that I was on the verge of a stunning breakthrough in vocal communication between *Homo sapiens* and a perfectly wild bird. Well, listen up.

I went down the path to the outhouse and stopped by a giant agave twenty feet from the partly open door. Because of the angle of the door and the site of the nest in a dark corner, there was no way that she could see or hear me. I waited, took a deep breath, and let out the call. Out she swooped. History had been made! The Bird Man of Alcazona had done it. I've never had to open the door since.

The story doesn't end there. The birdlets fledged and the nest grew empty. I hadn't minded sharing my privy for a month or so. But, frankly, it was good to be lavatorially free again.

After a few days I expected the wrens to demolish the nest, which, for some reason or other, they always do. Oddly, this didn't happen. Equally oddly, the birds seemed to be hanging 'round the old nest. A visiting guest, using my pastoral W.C. [water closet], reported seeing a bird on a nest. Oh, no, not that, I thought. Yes, defying all birdie lore, there were two more wren eggs. Was my outhouse turning into a den of wrens? Did they plan to populate me out of my own privy? The prospect was nightmarish.

Two days later, both pale-pink speckled eggs vanished, no bits of shell, not a trace of anything. Had the birds carried them off? They sometimes do. Had a snake slithered in for an eggs-over-easy breakfast? Oh, well, I murmured to myself, she raised five happily, enough for any one mother, surely? With a touch of wistfulness—for it had been a diverting and learning experience—I prepared to return to normality.

At the beginning of June the first egg of the third clutch was laid by what must be the horniest canyon wrens in the entire Southwest. There are now five. Mother and babies-to-be are doing well, thanks.

Geoffrey Platts, desert activist, is author of TREK! Man Alone in the Arizona Wild, a compilation of journals from his solitary journeys in the summertime Sonoran desert. He lives alone in a streamside cabin "somewhere in central Arizona" without electricity, telephone, car, fax, or wife. This wren story is from his 1994 journal.

Bird control

When last in Sun City, I found a quail's egg on the ground near my parents' home. My mother suggested I add it to a collection begun in my childhood in Galesburg, Illinois, where I was known as the bird boy. The egg collection still exists, cowbirds' and bluebirds' and sooty terns' eggs carefully blown and wrapped in cotton fuzz neatly packed into a green minnow bucket in the basement of a home in Detroit. I'm not sure what condition those eggshells are in, having experienced a flood. But I decided not to continue the collection by adding the quail's egg. The reason is guilt.

When I think about those thirty or forty eggs, I also think about the generations of birds that aren't with us today because I snatched from nests. There are enough natural enemies for birds; they didn't need me too. The collection grew in the early 1940s. Forty-five years later, the birds that might have survived had I not touched those eggs could be numbered in the thousands. At least, over these years, my consciousness has been raised. A reverence for life replaced a childish acquisitiveness.

Ecology

The morning paper July 19 tells of two Arizonans who won MacArthur fellowships. One prize, of $320,000, went to an ornithologist in Sedona, Marvin Philip Kahl, fifty-three. He photographs water birds. In the 1960s *National Geographic* sent him to Poland and Argentina to study storks. What became of that effort? Was it a backhanded way to delve into birth control? You've guessed now that Kahl's award burns me up. Someone else in Arizona should have received those 320,000 smackers from the foundation based on the late John D. MacArthur's real estate hoards: Eleanor Radke, the bird lady of Cave Creek.

Maybe she doesn't hold a PhD in birdwatching as does Kahl (actually, his is in zoology, a pretty big area), but Eleanor has done some things the MacArthur payoff guys aren't aware of. Such as a study of the Harris's hawk, in which she discovered the desert birds aren't as rare as some birdwatchers thought. And caring for sick and broken birds that people bring to her because she's of the same feather. She also has begun to rename birds to avoid sexism. Thus the female gila (pronounced *HE-luh*) woodpecker has become known to Eleanor as the shela (*SHE-luh*) woodpecker. She's toying with robinette and with scarlet ohara bird, the latter as a substitute for cardinal.

To make herself known to the boys at MacArthur who hand out the money each year, I propose that Eleanor undertake a simple study that might catch their attention. On a computer that sits in her husband Don's office, Eleanor could do a simulation of the events that would occur if quail had four or six legs. Those birds hoof it pretty well right now using two drumsticks. Imagine what they could do with more. Our local quail lives about a year and a half in the wild before something gets it. In a cage, the same quail might live to twenty years. Something clearly is wrong. I think it has to do with escaping mouths. Quail hate to fly. When they do, you hear a sound like that of horses neighing. They don't fly well. Maybe bigger wings would help. I think more legs might do it.

Of course, that brings up more questions. Could the quail's tiny brain coordinate the movement of more legs? And what would the extra speed do to coyotes, who love to take quail to lunch? Would these already lean doggy machines grow thinner in the faster chase? Might coyotes die out? That's what ecology is all about, considering what happens to everything around you when a species disappears or grows more dominant.

Eleanor, using Don's exotic computer, could find out.

I'd go after a MacArthur fellowship myself, but I understand they are not given to bird brains.

A single dove

As I came down the mountain from my evening walk, a dove dropped from a mesquite tree to the ground. I stopped, waiting for it to walk quickly away or fly up, but nothing moved. I peeked closer into tall weeds. It was a small mourning dove, probably out of the nest earlier this year. It seemed stuck in the weeds. Gently, slowly, I reached down and extracted it. The dove did not fly but sat in my hands. Some feathers missing left a bare, red breast. The bird breathed quickly but did not seem to mind my holding it. I put it in my straw hat and walked to the house. There I tried giving it water from an eye dropper, but it did not respond. After I ate my dinner I peeked in my hat again. The dove's beak was open, so I tried the water again. The water seemed to disappear into the beak. Then the dove's eyes closed and the head drooped. I scooped the bird out of the hat.

"Oh, no," I said to the dove, "are you going to leave us?" The breathing had stopped. The neck lay limp. What a beautiful creature, I thought, so complete, to grow from a small white egg into a wing-whistling, fast-flying sky scraper. I put the dove outside in the crotch of an old cherrywood log from Detroit. The evening coyote would find a warm meal.

5 May

That did not happen. Nor did it the next day. As of now, the dove's body has lain in the crotch of the stump for two days, touched only by the wind. No flies buzz around the corpse. No maggots work under the drying skin. What sends the message that this former bird is untouchable?

I want to hear "Pavane for a Dead Princess" echo across the valley. Does the death of the dove symbolize the death of peace? The wash has nearly dried up, the mountain drained of its winter substance. A mourning of doves is heard in our land.

6 May

She is risen. The dove has left her resting place. Not a feather is to be found. Doves perch on the power lines in pairs. They coo. They whistle as they fly. I look at each lone dove I see and wonder.

9 May

Sunday evening—seven—after my walk on the mountain, I turn on the road by the corrals and stop. Up the hill about fifty feet, staring back at me, is a mule deer. I stop. We eye each other for half a minute before the deer steps gracefully off the road and heads down the hill. She is followed by two more deer. Each stops and looks at me, ears quivering for something familiar. I wish them well, silently. They walk slowly off, stopping now and then to look back at me as I slowly walk up the road to the house.

Jane is missing this magical time. The palos verdes splash yellow on the green mountain. "I've never seen so much green," says DiBartolomeo, the architect-sculptor who renovates the former medical center across the valley.

At 7:30 I hear a loud thump, as if someone has slammed a door nearby, or, farther, something has blown up. I get up from the keyboard to explore and see nothing wrong. As I approach the house, the phone rings. Coming back up to the office I find the dead dove, its brains bashed out on the dark window it has flown into. It lies on its back, eyes shut forever, another messenger bearing a message I cannot or do not wish to read.

A stunning performance

Mark looked out the window. "A hummingbird just hit the window," he said. I had been working near the window but did not hear the thud. Mark kept looking.

"Is he out there?" I asked. I stood next to Mark and could see the shiny green jewel sitting on the ground, an unusual place for a hummingbird. We both watched the beak, a third the length of the body, twitch left and then right, a tiny conductor's baton directing a symphony of mosquitoes playing violins. At least the bird sat upright, not feet-up like a dead canary on the bottom of a cage.

The left and right turns of the bird's head increased. Maybe he was reprogramming the computer which had glitched when he hit the glass. In a moment, he shivered his feathers, such as they were, and buzzed straight off to a twig on an Arizona cypress ten feet away. We both cheered.

The maroon flash

Travelers to the tropics sometimes bring back stories of the green flash, a phenomenon rarely observed when the sun sets. Science has its explanations. I have been in the tropics but have yet to see the green flash. It sounds like a traffic light that spends most of its time red.

What I have seen in Arizona is the maroon flash. It happens on our porch every spring. Three wrought-iron lamps hang from beams under the ceiling out there. In March the house finches come to nest. The male comes emblazoned with maroon head and upper breast, as if he'd taken a dive part way into a paint bucket. He also brings the sweetest song a finch ever sang. Or so I think.

The sparrows like our lamps because the two working ones have missing glass panels. The birds bring twigs, twitter a lot, and seem to think the lamps would make fine homes for raising young. When I first noticed them there I was horrified and wanted to replace the missing glass panels. Messy birds splattering the porch with yesterday's lunch? Not here, thank you. And then I thought again. Sweet-singing birds. Fascinating creatures who have chosen our home for their short nesting season. We can watch the progress. Attitude is everything. Their kind probably have been nesting here since centuries before the house was built in 1951. Our kind intruded on their habitat. We have a chance to give some back. The lamp panels can wait.

Desert Sketchbook

An exam of the tail
  Of most cocky male Gambel's quail
Reveals this bumper-sticker try:
  "I'd rather run than fly!"

Your versatile cactus wren

Coming out of the back door on the way to the office I heard the bong-bong-bong of water falling from the roof's gutter onto a metal lid that doesn't quite cover the rain barrel. Because Arizona seemed poised to have one of its rare rainfalls, I walked to the barrel and flung off the cover, so that if more water fell, it could fill the barrel. Floating on the surface of the half-full barrel was what looked like a dead bird, in such disarray I could not guess the species. I felt badly for it, and resolved to fit the barrel with a screen so that personal disaster would not happen again. As I slid my hand under the bird, an eye opened, brown with a black center. It blinked. The bird miraculously was not dead.

As I scooped it from the water, its feet felt for and gripped my finger. The body shivered. The bird had given up body heat for who knows how long to the relatively cool water. In the house, I put the bird in a cardboard box, mixed some honey and water, and spooned the mixture into the bird's beak. The beak was long and curved, making me think this might have been an immature curve-billed thrasher. Except that the eye was not yellow. Maybe it was a cactus wren.

The bird wiggled its beak and got some of the sugar mixture down. The body, wrapped in wet feathers, still shook. Jane had just left for the store, leaving a hot oven where she'd conditioned a new cast-iron frying pan. I set the bird's box into the oven but kept the door open. The heat seemed to restore some vigor to the bird. After a few minutes, I pulled it out of the oven and fed it some more honey water, then made a nest of a dish towel and set the bird in a basket over the sink. (The Bird Lady of Cave Creek says giving an injured bird any liquid "is not a good idea for novices." After all, this wren had just tried to swallow a barrelful.)

After an hour at my desk, I returned to the kitchen to check on the patient. As I entered, the alarmed bird, perched on the edge of the nest and now almost dry, leaped and flew across a foot of space and clung, woodpeckerlike, to a steel bar on the window. It was clear the patient was ready to leave. I grabbed it, recognized now in preened state a cactus wren, stepped to the door, and opened my hand. The young bird flew about ten feet, then walked up Jim Hill and hid under a bush. I hoped it would not now fall prey to its other enemies, snake, coyote, or bobcat.

The curiosity-driven wren clan has found its way into the truck through barely-open windows. I found one once where usually packrats only go, under the hood of the truck. And on one terrible morning a few years back, when I failed to hide the packrat trap, a stiff wren sat spread-eagled, squashed by a powerful spring, its silent beak in peanut butter. But the rain barrel incident was the first time I'd seen a cactus wren play duck.

Lovey dovey

Anyone with ears who inhabits North America knows the soft cooing call of doves. I heard them first in Illinois, as a child, followed them to Michigan, and now find they're nesting on my porch in Arizona. They are mourning doves, given that name by popular demand for the human-interpreted cooing they produce. At least I now know why they do it.

Doves aren't thrashers or mockingbirds. Doves don't have the great range of repertoire of those other multi-throated birds. They coo.

Lately a male has perched on a dead agave stalk we have tied to the chimney. He coos occasionally. My testosterone-flavored head tells me he's soliciting any females in the area: *Hey, I'm here. I'm ready. Come flash your tail.*

Maybe with age my glands have let my reason return. I just realized why he's cooing. His wife sits quietly on their nest between roof and beam at a corner of our west-facing porch. He's assuring her that he's handy, that everything's okay. She doesn't answer back, either because she doesn't have the vocal equipment to do so or because she's smart enough not to attract attention to her nest. Maybe she sends him thought patterns: *How about a nice juicy cricket? I sure could use one of them.* Or, *How about spelling me for a while so I can get a drink?* Or, *Have you swept the back porch yet?*

At Quistamos, we are awaiting the hatch of two more dove mouths to feed all the while listening to the soothing sound of Father Dove.

How the owl came to be

The rodents got smart. Hawks were picking them off from high above. "We'll go nocturnal," the rodents decided, and fell asleep until night came. Then the hawks couldn't see them. The hawks went hungry until they realized what those nasty mice and rats had done. A venturesome band of hawks decided they could play the same game. They became owls.

An environmental impact statement for right-wing bird lovers

Thanks to a gift from Nancy, we've been putting out birdseed, attracting a variety of fine-feathered friends and several squirrels. (I tried planting some of the birdseed, but only English sparrows and starlings came up.)

Pecking at the living room window now are flickers, curved-billed thrashers, quail, towhees, mourning doves, and white-crowned sparrows. Mark reported a sapsucker. At night, mice emerge from the bush to stuff cheeks with what the birds have spilled and what the day squirrels (Harris's and ground) have overlooked. It's been Fat City around our place for the past few weeks.

One day while watching the feast framed by the window, I thought of the implications. While those birds quaffed down easily-got seed, insects they usually eat declared a holiday from fear. To the joy of the bugs, the birds had gone vegetarian. I imagined cockroaches, spiders, and flies proliferating while the birds gave them up for easier stuff. I imagined the birds growing unhealthy because I'd altered their diets. Maybe the bugs' adrenal glands withered from disuse. "No more fright! No more need for flight!" I could imagine them chorusing.

Then I remembered reading about how it isn't hard-hearted not to put out water for birds. (We do that, too.) A water basin becomes a germ factory. Doves are particularly susceptible. A parasite creates an infection. Tissues in the throat swell. Air to the lungs stops. The dove dies, sometimes in mid-flight.

What ecological horrors have I created playing philanthropist with birdseed?

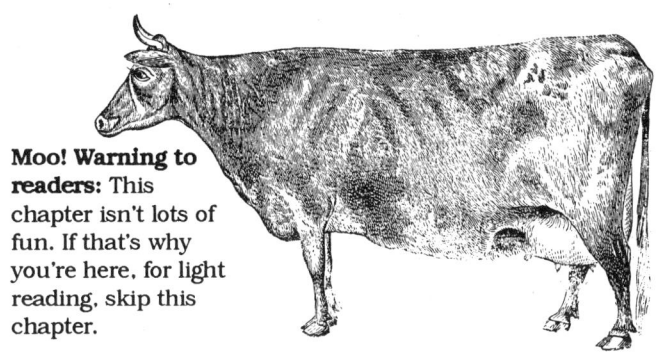

Moo! Warning to readers: This chapter isn't lots of fun. If that's why you're here, for light reading, skip this chapter.

Battle with cattle

How to turn a problem into a new sport

With a little cattle-prodding from a couple of shy Earth First!ers, I checked recently with the Cave Creek district of the Tonto National Forest, that big chunk of Arizona north of where I live. The Earth First! folks hinted that maybe Desert Mountain Properties, a big development northeast of town, ran a cattle herd. I thought their premise outrageous: that for the sake of a tax break or for a fresh supply of beef for its banquet tables, Desert Mountain actually kept cattle.

Turns out that's exactly what Desert Mountain does, even while draining our aquifer of a million gallons a day to water its three eighteen-hole golf courses. The cattle do not graze on the fairways, though. They're carefully controlled just to the north, in the national forest, one of eleven herds permitted to cause erosion and trample delicate desert within the Cave Creek district.

Patti R. Fenner, who handles permits for the Forest Service, told me about the cattle. The herd includes sixty-five head, but there may be more than four times hooves than heads, because a calf and its mother cow count as one head or, in Forest Service lingo, animal unit. Bully for them.

Why would Desert Mountain maintain a herd? I naively asked.

"That's a question we don't ask," said Ms. Fenner. "We only issue permits."

"You mean I could get a permit to allow my cattle to ravage the national forest—if I had cattle?" I naively asked.

Ms. Fenner said I could run my cattle—but not anything about ravaging—when a permit became available. I could buy an existing herd and take over its permit. She supposed that Desert Mountain got its permit when it bought what had been known as Carefree Ranch, about 8,600 acres which actually held cattle during the days of the wild west, when land was cheap here.

The discussion made me wonder if a millionaire of Carefree, geriatrically gifted, as they say in Sun City, might want to buy a herd in the national forest and become a permittee. He could then give the cattle to those unhealthy people still eating them—kids in the public school cafeterias and the homeless—and continue to pay his little permit fee each year, supporting a ghost herd. The price is $1.81 per month per animal unit, subject to change March 1. So desert destruction comes pretty cheaply.

Wouldn't work, says Ms. Fenner. You need real hooves scraping away real plants.

I'm not so sure. The Forest Service is known to bend to every whim of vested interests which want to use or desecrate what the public owns, allowing mining, ranching, camping, off-road vehicle, and almost any other form of desert rape. (A wonderful exception is Delvin R. Lopez, new district ranger for Cave Creek and sensitive to environmental concerns.)

I'll see if the men and women in olive green will accept embalmed cattle, which, from a distance will look alive and destructive. If so, maybe we can find sponsors for these ghost herds and permit the forest to begin to return to its natural state, a process which will take centuries but for which our descendants will thank us.

In the meantime, Thomas H. Blaney, Cave Creek's photographer-recyclist-environmentalist, has suggested a new sport which offers to solve several environmental problems at once:

"I propose," Tom writes, "...a new sport...uniquely Arizonan in character [that] would more than make up for the Super-Bowl [lost because Arizona at that time did not have a paid holiday honoring the late Rev. Martin Luther King]...

"ORVs [off-road vehicles] would race over obstacle courses occupied by teams of camouflaged survivalists armed with paint bullets, while guerilla golfers try to play through undisturbed. The possibilities of combinations and strategies are endless.

"A statewide contest could be held to select a name for the sport and adopt rules and scoring. I guarantee it would be an instant success and become a new national pastime.

"As inventor of the sport, I suggest the name Bonzo-Bike-Bullet-Ball, subject, of course, to a vote of the people. I predict, though, that it will eventually be known as National Forest 2050."

Tom's idea is not so far out. Richard (*Jonathan Livingston Seagull*) Bach, in his book *The One*, visualized a new international sport to replace war. In some future time, piston-engined biplanes would shoot at each other with laser beams, activating smoke bombs with every strike. Almost every nation could field teams that would provide excitement seen by TV cameras mounted on the planes. A world series could be just that. If Tom's idea happens first, I'd be just as happy.

I'd give up beef for that.

To solve many problems, make a few simple changes

Doctors and the medical news media tell us, contrary to what the Beef Council tells us, that we should eat less red meat. Even the leanest cut of beef still holds forty per cent fat. That's problem one.

Problem two came to my attention during an Earth Day rally, when Steve Jones raised my consciousness about cattle grazing free in our national forests, and of the terrible destruction they cause.

Hunters express frustration lately over less game to shoot. Deer, elk, and bear seem to be disappearing, not to mention our mountain lions. That's problem three.

The last, obvious problem is water. It's disappearing faster than the wildlife, what with heavy use by golf courses.

So I thought of a few simple fixes for all of those problems.

We declare open season on cattle in the national forests. For a week, anyone could drive in and bag himself a mean bull or a fecund cow, shoot it from his vehicle if he wishes, butcher it on the spot, and drive off with a bloody hind or front lashed on the hood. How macho. What a saving of money for meat, for the good of our national forests.

The US Department of Agriculture, of which the Forest Service is but a branch on the tree of government, would compensate the ranchers for the loss of their herds, of course. And how fitting it would be, much like the government paying poor farmers in Virginia to grow death-dealing tobacco. Imagine all of that cholesterol disappearing.

The hunters wouldn't get all of the cattle, of course. The surviving bovines could be gathered up by ranch owners in a final herd round-up that would rival anything Hollywood could produce. With cowboys yelling, dogs barking, and national forest dust flying, the herds would be driven down to our communities, to the water-gulping golf courses. There the cattle could spend their last days nibbling the fairways and plunging hoof deep into the soft greens, wallowing in the sand traps, fattening up for their final trip.

Sometimes simple ideas can solve major problems. It's about time we started.

A cure for hoof in mouth disease

One of the issues you find in Arizona but not in most other states is the legal grazing of cattle on public lands. If that is all that cattle do—graze—they might prove tolerable. Unfortunately, cattle hooves destroy terrain and habitat. Cattle output pollutes what poor streams we have. The presence of cattle discourages humans from using the land for legitimate recreational purposes.

The cattlemen argue that's the way the Old West has always been, at least since they got rid of the sheep. Tradition, if nothing reasonable, should dictate that cattle keep slurping at the public trough.

What's too bad is that the US Forest Service officially supports the cattle interests. It has become an apologist for them. David F. Jolly, Southwestern regional forester, published a white paper dated January 11, 1991, that is a thinly-veiled public relations campaign in favor of cattle interests. One of his arguments is "Old West traditionalism."

I suppose you could argue that tradition favors tobacco smoking, never mind what the surgeon general has said. Yet our society has turned away from that diseased thinking. It is turning away from unhealthy beef, too. Beef, with no cut of meat less than forty per cent fat, is not healthy for human hearts. Medical science agrees. Nowhere in Jolly's paper does he mention anything about the human cost of taking those cattle to market, yet eating the cows is a factor.

Beef cattle may have contributed heavily to the economy of the Old West. Jolly claims they may have a $68 million effect on Arizona's economy alone. He never hints at the larger cost of fat-induced cancer and heart diseases.

Our society turns away from red meat for many reasons. Will the Forest Service, hanging onto an unhealthy past, be the last to awake to the reality of tomorrow? Invading Americans shot the last buffalo on the plains before the turn of the century. Who will kill the last cow?

A letter to the local Smokey

Dear Ranger Lopez:

Only in this week's *Foothills Sentinel* did I note your request for comments on the Seven Springs recreation area. I've just picked up a copy of your form letter, #1910, and it notes that you'd like comments by 30 April. I hope this is not too late.

My comments may seem facetious, but these are deadly serious.

I say, develop the hell out of Seven Springs. Put in a superhighway to get the citizens to the area. Give them every kind of facility they might like, including Smokey Bear robots. The point: Keep the uninformed forest visitor confined so he won't further destroy the forest. If he's happy at Seven Springs with his pop machines and a place to ride his ATV, maybe he'll stay away from what needs conserving around here, the desert.

You ask if there are "any potential partners willing to share the expenses of constructing and maintaining this area with the Forest Service?" Yes, I'm willing to set up a jeep or tour bus service to bring members of the National Rifle Association and others into your forest on daily cattle hunts. Dressed in camouflage, we'd roam the desert roads looking for cattle. For each one shot, we'd butcher the carcass and operate a little shop in the back of the bus where our pro butchers would reduce the animal to freezer packages by the time the bus returned to Seven Springs, where the bones could be left for visitors' dogs or soup. The business would self-destruct after a few months, I'm afraid, but running it would provide fun for me, beef on the tables of people who don't know better, and, best of all, would slim down or eradicate the worst scourge now at work in our forests—since few cuttable trees exist in the Tonto.

Please let me know when I can buy and outfit the bus. I'm raring to go.

Arrest them cows! For obscenity, of course

Sheriff Joe Arpaio has his posse's work cut out for him. The amateurs quickly rid Phoenix of its most visible prostitutes. How do you follow that kind of success? What can sustain a major public-spirited effort that involves the citizens but doesn't trip over the line into anarchy?

I think I have it. Arrest the cows in the national forests.

Arizona obscenity statutes define as obscene "explicit materials involving e———-t," according to Rick Romley's special assistant, Barnett Lotstein, quoted in the December 2 *Arizona Republic*. (The *Republic* could use the *e* word, but it is too nasty for the *Sentinel*. Hint: Robin Williams in the movie "Dead Poets Society" uses the *e* word to his class of boys when characterizing formulas applied to poetry.

(The *Sentinel* is so sacrosanct about bodily functions that it doesn't even provide t. p. for its employees. To do so would admit to their baser natures. About eight years ago one of its subscribers complained in a letter to the editor about my use of the word *crud*. So miffed was he that he moved to a small town in northern Arizona where he could not be assaulted by bad words in weekly newspapers; the town had no newspaper.)

But cows do it, apparently without the slightest concern for who's watching or when or where they let go. Some western towns even have contests involving cows. Walk them up the street and where they emit, the merchant with the closest store to the scene wins some contest. And rushes out with broom and shovel, no doubt.

Before you rush out to wrap your cows' hinds in skirts so they—you—don't violate the

The blind squirrel & other Arizona animal tails

Arizona statutes, that isn't enough. Just finding the evidence on the ground is all the grounds needed for an indictment.

The sheriff's posse could exercise their lassos and ride into the Tonto to arrest those d———g cows, then haul them down to headquarters for grilling, preferably medium rare.

But the effort would have to be fair. A judge would have to hear or smell the evidence, listen to some witnesses, before placing his order to the chef.

Oh, s——.

For subjects scatological
It's only cattle-logical:
To keep our forests green,
Install an abattoir machine.

Let virtual cows roam the range

Dear Delvin Lopez,

You've asked again for public comment on doings in your Tonto National Forest. The Cartwrights have been running cattle north of Cave Creek for 99 years, I understand. That makes that family wholly responsible—plus the Forest Service for helping them do it—for the degradation of the land in the huge acreage that spills over into Yavapai County.

55,718 acres. Incredible. Lots of folks think the Cartwrights are some television-series family, and they may be, but they're also local and have been since the end of the last century. They're a part of Cave Creek's history. It's time that history ended and a new tradition of caring for the public lands began.

You seem to suggest in your request to the public for comments that there may be a number of reasons to keep the Cartwright disease from spreading. One is the threat to endangered species impacted by the miserable cattle. That's reason enough. I'll suggest some ways here that will help the Forest Service people who know the score and who sympathize with those of us who don't think cows should occupy public lands. I know, you have to write all those fancy words and remain detached and not let on to your own opinions, but I can read between the lines. Here are some grounds to get rid of the cows.

Religious. Let's get the fundamentalist preachers to give hellfire-and-brimstone sermons. Point out that the devil has come to the national forest and is rapidly reproducing himself. Doesn't the devil have hooves and horns? Sounds like a cow to me. Preach eradication by any means. Put the devil back in Hell. (Oh, Lordy!)

Second amendment. Besides protecting our right to keep and arm bears, the National Rifle Association can recommend to its members that they test their hardware every weekend or so by firing at slow-moving four-footed beasts. Try different ammo to see what goes all the way through the middle. What kind of exit hole does it leave? Do some original research. And do it soon, before the Left takes away those guns. A cow a day keeps the Clintons away.

Computer science. To solve the problem of sustaining tradition, I suggest we get rid of the real cows, replacing them with virtual cows. Virtual reality is big now and growing, just like a pregnant cow. For those who miss the home on the range, let them explore the national forest via computer with helmet, gloves, and imagination. Keep a little manure around to clinch the effect. Result: Prevents virtual species, the result of extinction.

"Where never is heard a discouraging word—

What the hell can a dead bullock say?"

Health. Every nutritionist knows that the leanest cut of beef contains at least forty percent fat. Even medical doctors know that animal fat turns into Drano-proof linings in veins and arteries, leading to heart disease and stroke. Doing away with those cows does beef eaters a favor. We can still have cattle in the national forest, but they can be made of soy bean meal and run around on little wheels, leaving nothing behind and not pawing up delicate washes and streambeds.

Economy. Send those cows to Japan to balance the trade deficit. Beef fat is better than nothing. Morally wrong? American tobacco companies don't mind selling their death-dealing products increasingly abroad as Americans wise up.

Yours for a wiser, smarter, healthier, more pristine national park where all the people, not just ranchers, can play.

Other cattle costs

Beef and other livestock cost eight times more grain to create than if people ate the grain. Animals also cost almost fifty percent of our agricultural energy use from factory farm to mouth, according to Lizz Grenard. Seventy per cent of grain grown in the USA goes to feed livestock, according to *State of the World, 1992.*

—Jane E. Grenard

Coyote voice

Twelve thirty-six.

A lone coyote yowls. All over town dog throats vibrate at a low pitch. Growls.

Peg comforts. "Hush, Watson. It's all right."

Charlie cuts off Bimbo by just thinking of The Stick.

Joseph reaches a hand down from the bed and pats Joshua's muzzle. The growl dies.

For fifteen minutes the coyote sings, now up, now down the valley, now high and wavering, now low and bark-like.

"Yip, yip, whoeeeeeeee."

No one answers. The moon is down.

The developers have come.

About those coyote voices

I've had a request from a former Arizonan now suffering from terminal cloudiness in Michigan. She'd like me to record our twice-daily concerts of coyotes and send her a tape.

Well, I set out to do that with the latest in hi-tech gear, a microphone as accurate as a rifle, coupled to a vest-pocket recorder. She'd get the highest fi while listening to the shaggy beasts gargle among the boulders behind our place.

Trouble is that coyotes are smarter than we think. They're also hams. When they saw what I was doing—from at least 300 feet away—they sent a representative with a white flag. I got the message quickly enough: No dogfood, no sing-sing.

Trouble was that the store was out of canned dog food, and I wasn't about to buy a big bag just to get them to loosen up their throats, so I substituted canned cat food.

Big mistake. Through the telescope I could see them wolf down the stuff, tossing the empty cans in the air. Recorder and mike stood by, ready for their short concert.

Unfooled, they meowed like kitty cats.

The next day I brought three cans of the real stuff, emptied it into a big bowl, and left the cans so that the coyotes could see pictures of their doggy brothers on the labels. This worked. They started yowling even before I got back to the mike and the recorder.

Over time our symbiosis became more social. I have on tape almost a full hour of coyote voices, the last few minutes the most spectacular of all: They sing the national anthem, and far better than does that bombastic butterball on television. Maybe they'll consent to open a few ball games if rehearsals go well.

Why coyotes yowl

In this green valley where we live surrounded by Black Mountain and the towns of Cave Creek and Carefree, we hear coyotes yowl in chorus at least once a day. Often their singing comes just before or just after sunset. Sometimes it happens as a full moon rises, sometimes a bit before dawn. We hear them so often, so clearly, that we know instantly what it is thatcomes across the valley or up from the wash to our ears. Yet each time there is a fraction of a second of terror when we tighten our bodies before relaxing with recognition. If you've never heard a coyote express himself verbally, you have in store for you a grand introduction to the Old West. Sure, coyotes adapt to cities, and probably can be heard in the likes of Los Angeles and Nogales. Out here, though, their yowling reminds us of the thinness of our civilization: Not much stands between us and the primeval desert.

    And what sounds. We've heard the canids scream, cry like babies, and caterwaul like cats. When I first heard them, on my move to the Sonoran desert, I thought a bunch of rowdy high school boys was trying to stimulate the local dog population the way a siren does.

Why coyotes make the noises they do isn't clear to me. I've speculated on the subject, as a good amateur archaeologist might speculate on the use of a tool found at a site. Like Edmund Rostand's Cyrano de Bergerac, I've cataloged the possible reasons for the coyotes' unique behavior.

Forgetful: The sun sinks, and it might not remember to come back tomorrow.

Terrifying: These sounds will let the lesser creatures of the desert know their places.

Celebratory: I've just caught dinner, and you can't have any.

Paranoid: I know you're out there, but you'd better not come close to me.

Primal: Another day is done, we've survived it, and I just have to tell you about the time—.

Releasing: It's a crummy life, and I need to get this off my chest (or fur).

Generous: There's this flock of quail, and I'm driving them over your way for supper.

If coyotes could speak our language, these are things they might say. They can't, of course, so I try to speak for them, knowing I could be a million miles off their intent. As common as they are—have the yellow eyes of one never caught in your headlights?—coyotes keep a great secret we cannot seem to learn.

One morning Jane and I looked down the hollow at what first appeared to be five playful dogs frolicking on a two-decades-old dry manure pile. Tail wagging, one tossed a white object, a cloth or a bird, to another. One coyote put his head down and plowed it through the dusty brownness. Then they heard or saw us. Tails went between legs. We saw them for what they were. And then we didn't see them. They evaporated into the surrounding brush, becoming coyotes again.

Maybe in their wailing the coyotes are trying to tell us something that they know: That we who disturb the desert so grandly are ruining it for everyone who lives here, coyote and canary alike. Maybe their sad songs cry out for the way the desert was before roads and houses and golf courses. Maybe the yowling is a note of disgust at what wise man does to foul his own nest. Maybe the coyotes sense it even if we do not.

A coyote voice continues

Cave Creek writer Vikki Auten warns against feeding the wildlife, and with good reason. The animals should not depend on their chief enemy for anything. Sometimes, though, such feeding may be justified.

He sniffed around our garbage dump last fall. We called him The Young Coyote because that's obviously what he was, a junior version of the yellow-gray hides that hang around our valley despite the continuous building program of *Homo sapiens dope-us*. The young guy was smaller than the others, nimble, solitary.

One day in January we saw him limping. Out the bedroom window we could see his wound, a red chunk left in his upper left foreleg that looked as if someone had taken a grinding wheel to it. His yellow eyes looked at us through the window, perhaps thanking us for what we threw out, perhaps asking for Grey Poupon on the turkey next time.

We didn't see the young coyote for some weeks. When we did, it was in mid-February down by the hay barn. He'd been sunning on the thick, high grass that follows rain. His wound, carefully and often licked, was more brown than red and seemed to be healing. But what was this? Now he limped on the other leg, too. Did he get it caught in a trap? Step on a thorn he couldn't pull out? When he ratcheted up from resting to run from us, the slow painful movement caught our empathy. This coyote was dying. He looked ragged and thin. With two forelegs not functioning well, he couldn't chase down food.

I immediately went up to the house and brought an opened can of salmon. The coyote let me come within about thirty feet, but then limped off. I set the open can on a flat rock and retreated. The next day Mark visited. After telling him about the coyote, he took an open can of tuna. If he had not been ostracized already, the coyote's fellows now would surely avoid him for fishy breath.

Two days later the coyote appeared at our dump. He limped horribly, barely able to stand. We gave him more salmon and some fresh-baked bread. His yellow eyes at the window seemed to say, "Don't forget the Grey Poupon." For a week, we made sure the coyote ate well. He grew more mobile, less pained when he walked. He was recovering. He'd also lost much of his fear of us; we could approach within ten feet now. He knew we were friends who for some reason were helping him. When presenting him with a can of fish, I would squat in order to appear less threatening, hold out the can, and then back away. The coyote watched, wanting to come closer but resisting the feeling. I wanted to hold his hurt paw and heal it, to brush his fur, but I also wanted to allow him his wildness.

For two days we did not see the coyote. Had he been killed in a fight? Recovered, had he moved to new territory?

One night near the end of March we arrived home after dark. The house loomed black-dark, half surrounded by a moonless sky full of stars, the lights out. On the way to the front door, stepping carefully and using a flashlight, we caught a rabbit in the beam. It lay against a corner of the house, freshly killed. The rabbit had not died of cardiac arrest or bad arteries; blood splattered the bricks around it. Why would a rabbit get killed on our porch—and then get left by its killer?

Lessons from childhood came back. Pet cats and dogs sometimes brought tokens of their love to doorsteps, still-live mice or baby birds, expressions of their love, grisly as they were. Had the young coyote, grateful for his caregivers, brought a present? And offered proof of his recovery?

When Pavlov's dog meets Schödinger's cat

Everyone who has approached the subject of psychology has learned of Ivan Petrovich Pavlov (1849-1936), the Russian physiologist who taught dogs to ring a bell if they wanted to eat. We had a demonstration of the effect at our home last week. It proved that sound scientific principles can be shown by anyone at any time, even in reverse order.

We'd been feeding a limping coyote for more than a month, putting out cans of salmon and tuna, practically handing him slices of bread. Both of his forelegs had been damaged somehow. His limp was so bad he could hardly stand, let alone run to catch dinner.

Over that month the coyote's ability to walk increased, we were glad to see. Still, he came around to feed. Still, we handed out goodies, though we told ourselves we honestly tried to wean him of human contact.

One evening our coyote friend returned to our patio with some of his friends, about six yellow dogs in all. He led the entourage, limping slightly. The other five coyotes limped, too. We watched through the window, amazed. Had our friend become a pied piper of wounded coyotes?

In a second, we realized the awful truth. His friends had learned from his behavior how to bilk our cabinets. He'd taught us to ring his bells.

Shaggy dogs & real

The dog who never sleeps... and other domesticated-mammalian tales

Mr. Sniffs Goes to Dawglington

Down the road comes Mr. Sniffs,
Nose to ground like Sherlock's hound,
Checking out even old whiffs,
Hunting clues where're they're found.

He's solved crimes, found lost men,
And all with the use of nose.
So sensitive, super-ken,
Mr. Sniffs is big on rose.

They say he sniffed Hohokam,
What the ancient had to eat,
The meal gone five-hundred years
And without a whiff of meat.

No man could come with such nose,
It's as true as London fog.
Mr. Sniffs agrees with those
Who recognize him as Dog.

Living with a rat fink

*F*or a month now we've enjoyed the company of someone we'd been told was a dog, a schnauzer, in fact. He certainly looks like such a dog. He can do a good imitation of a bark and a snarl. Tramp has learned well. But, as Lloyd Bentsen once said of a competing candidate, "I knew dogs, and, frankly, you ain't no dog." Or something like that. Tramp is not a dog at all but a capybara.

The only reason we know is because Jim Hill sold me a bottleful of ginkgo capsules. Extract from the ancient tree is supposed to increase circulation (I should use it on my newsletters) and improve memory. After a month of downing the gelcaps, I've found my memory incredibly improved. Thus, exposure of the dog-rat.

I recalled a picture in my book of New World mammals, last looked at fifty years ago when given to me by my parents when they were young. Because my memory is now so good, I cracked open the thick book to the right page. There was a picture of Tramp. The caption, though, identified the beast as a capybara, a South American river rat and the world's largest rodent.

(Separately, Jane wonders what the Germans bred schnauzers to do. The dogs are too small to hunt except for rodents. I suggested the original purpose may have been to provide schnauzer schnitzels when other meat supplies ran low.)

How Tramp learned to mimic a schnauzer and how he arrived in Arizona, I have no idea, but a mere dog Tramp is not. We have confirmation of that fact from a Hopi chieftain who called on us one afternoon. In between Tramp's barks, the Native American managed to say, "What are you doing with a capybara?" He recognized the hidden rat in dog's fur at first glance. "Let me guess," he added. "His name is He Who Pees on the Floor."

"How do you know all these things?" I asked.

"I have great memory," the chief said. "Remember everything I see and read."

"Photographic memory is a mark of genius," I pontificated.

"No genius," he said, blushing. "I take ginkgo

capsules. You can get them at the Blue Bird."

Before the rat goes back to his family on the other side of the mountain, I intend to pee on his leg, just to get even.

Reader dogs for the blind

No, I don't mean *leader* dogs. The idea came to me that dogs, as intelligent as they are, might read to their blind masters if only they possessed the right equipment, a set of vocal chords from a recently-killed human. So I'm suggesting this concept to the medical folks who like to experiment with dogs. Besides tissue rejection, they'd have to overcome other obstacles, such as how to prevent singing in the shower, or the use of fowl language in a barnyard, or a proclivity toward alcoholic beverages by the new throat's owner. But medical science has made great leaps, and maybe the time is right to attempt this breakthrough. If you don't think I'm serious, let's hear a big arf-arf.

The operation

Our daughter Lizz, the veterinarian-in-training, drove down from Fort Collins, Colorado, recently to perform a practice operation on the female dog she gave her grandparents for Christmas. The dog, a sad-eyed elfin semi-pit bull, had been in heat. Lizz and I conferred first by phone. I bought the necessary supplies: surgical sponges, cat gut, and bandaging materials. I'd asked Lizz if we'd need duct tape, since ducts were what we'd be working on.

The phone went dead for a moment. Lizz was thinking. "I don't think so, but you might bring your stapler. We could use that instead of sutures." She's quick, our daughter.

Lizz arrived with borrowed tools: scalpel, spreaders, clamps, needles, and a tiny vial of ether. She wanted to see if she could make Tigger throw up after the operation.

With my parents watching, Lizz and I strapped on masks, gassed the dog, and then stretched her out on their kitchen table. The ether seemed to flow out of Tigger's lungs as she breathed. Grandpa held a spotlight for as long as he could, then passed it to Grandma when he had to go outside for air. Tigger never threw up, but Grandpa did.

Lizz worked quickly and efficiently. I'd shaved the dog's abdomen an hour before, and Lizz sliced through it, making a bloodless incision. I tried not to interrupt, but I couldn't help speaking a *National Enquirer* headline that came to mind:

MIRACLE DOG LIVES 6 MONTHS WITHOUT KIDNEYS

Lizz didn't think that was funny, but Grandpa laughed so hard he had to go outside again.

After Lizz got her gloved hand inside Tigger's tummy, the blood started to leak out. I kept busy mopping away until the sponges were used up.

"How about some paper towels?" I asked Grandma.

"We're out."

"How about some bath towels?"

"In the laundry room, Edward."

Edward was out, buying a newspaper. When he came in, I ripped it out of his hands and stuffed it around the pale carcass of a dog.

Lizz felt for a pulse in Tigger's throat.

"Weak," she reported, "but still there. I'll have to work fast."

"Please do," said Edward, heading for the door again.

Lizz pulled something out of the abdomen and tied it off. I reminded her that her grandfather had asked for the giblets. He's a gourmet cook if not a vegetarian.

Soon Lizz zipped along the incision, her needle and cat gut flying.

"Do you use dog gut on cats?" I asked.

Lizz finished just in time. Tigger was coming out of the ether, blinking her eyes, rolling her head. Lizz swabbed the closed wound with alcohol, patted Tigger on the head, and gave the dog an injection.

"What's that?" I asked.

"A little testosterone. Without ovaries Tigger won't make any of her own— Did I say *testosterone*? I meant estrogen!" Lizz looked at the syringe as if it had made a mistake. "Oh, well."

"This was a practice operation, anyway," I soothed.

In a few hours Tigger returned to her feet and walked at the end of a leash outside. It took a week for her to begin chasing quail again, but she healed quickly. Her abdominal scar disappeared.

Three sequelae (as doctors like to call them) happened, though. Inspired by Lizz's work, I rented space in an office building and opened a Sun City branch of Planned Parenthood. Roman Catholics who had been picketing the film *The Last Temptation of Christ* covered their signs with new messages about right to life and anti-abortion and picketed my parents' home in Sun City. And poor Tigger grew excess facial hair and began to bark in a much deeper voice.

Lizz is back in Fort Collins, taking a course in hormonology. I'd sure like to assist at her next operation.

To teach a dog to bark

I've been having cruel fun with Geoffrey Platts, taunting him about his *bête noire,* in this case a *bête* brown, a puppy bought late last year by one of Geoffrey's neighbors, Linda Lebeau, the exerciser. Jane and I take yoga lessons from her. Linda, the good mother, brought her new dog to class, keeping him in the car in a cage—until he outgrew the cage.

For a name for the dog, I suggested Geoffrey, or more modernly, Jeffrey. Linda toyed with that idea for a while, then named her mutt Odie, for some comic strip character. Odie started small. His huge feet portended a giant dog. And so it came to pass. He would not fit in the cage and soon not even in Linda's little Saab.

One day, when the dog was still of manageable size and looking back at me from the driver's seat of Linda's car as I breezed in to the yoga class, I noticed something. I'd never heard Odie bark. He was good at whining, but no healthy barks came from his massive jaws. I gave Linda some advice:

"When you raise a dog away from other dogs, he won't learn to bark unless you teach him."

Linda spotted that leg-pull as soon as it slipped out of my mouth and began laughing.

"I bark at Odie every time I pass your car," I said, doing a good imitation of what dogs do, vocally. Barking, we both knew, was at the expense of one Geoffrey Platts, who dislikes the sound of dogs even more than the sight.

Last year I told Geoffrey about a soundless dog I'd seen in Prescott. The little bitch could only hiss; some veterinarian had done a snip-snip job on nerves leading to its larynx. That was Geoffrey's kind of dog, a Victorian child, seen and not heard.

Then Monday, as we rushed late into yoga class, we saw in Linda's car no cage, no dog, just the shredded leather upholstery of her car seats.

"Where's Odie?" we asked, both Jane and I.

"He's back at my cabin, tearing it up," she said.

"You should have left him with Geoffrey as a sitter."

That was the first thing I said. The second was in response to kind words from a white-haired woman I'd never seen before but who seemed to remember me:

"I've told my husband about you," she said. "How you'd be a great golfer because you do yoga."

It was obvious to me later that she'd rehearsed that line to make it sound authentic; she was being nice to me, the only male in the class. But I slapped her in the face with this:

"There's no place for golf in the desert." I was quoting Geoffrey Platts, automatically, without thinking through the haze of 0745 on a Monday.

Later, I realized what had happened. Geoffrey had taught me to bark.

The Dog Haters' Handbook

I propose to Geoffrey Platts that he collaborate with me on a book with the title above. (Subtitle: *Get a new leash on life without dogs.*) It should sell well. There are far more dog-haters in America than solitary trekkers. Geoffrey may not want to come aboard, because, as he recently wrote to me, he doesn't dislike dogs, just their barking. Maybe he could contribute a chapter on what's irritating about having your meditation—or sleep—shattered by a dog whose throat never grows sore.

Many are the reasons not to like dogs. Geoffrey and I could implore newspaper editors and postal carriers across the country to send us clippings on dog damage: tots ravaged by doggie teeth—"Don't worry. He never bites"—and the poverty-stricken kept down by the need to buy dog food. How many billions of dollars do Americans spend on food for Fifi? Those are only starters. Consider the myriad of diseases helped along by what supposedly is man's best friend. Dogs bring the bugs home in fur and feces, in urine and saliva, loving you all the way to the hospital, unaware of their host relationship to some vicious parasites.

Most of all, though, dogs soak up affection, love better spent on people by people. Maybe I'm just jealous.

Letters from a dog

29 July 1994

Dear Amelia,

This is your dog barking. I mean, talking. I mean, writing. Jak, with his new computer, has been able to translate what I woof into words that I mean.

I MISS YOU!!

But I like it here, so don't spend a cat's hair worrying about me. And don't come back so soon. Jak and Jane are teaching me new trix. Like not to look back when I fart. They taught me to wrinkle my nose and look at someone else when I fart. If there's a cat in the room, I'm to look at the cat and wrinkle my nose.

They're also doing what they call a gut purge. I think they may be trying to convert me to vegetarianism, because I've been eating overripe bananas since you left. The taste is wonderful, much better than that awful "dogfood" you give me. I also had some

woof, woof, arghh, woof

rice and some funny kind of bean. [Sometimes the machine doesn't work, thus the interruption. —Ed.]

My summer friends have taught me a song from a musical called *Gulls and Dogs*. I'll wail it for you when you get back—or when you call from the great cold country.

When you see a dog
Jumping high like a frog,

Well, you know that he's doin' it for some cat.
Bark it woof, bark it woow-ee,
This is surely no cow-ee,
And that dog's only doin' it for some cat.
Bark to you later.
—Tramp the Arfmaster

(Transliterated by Professor Arnold H. Schwartzman)

Horses

My horse healed me
Copyright © 1995 by Julie Alex-Rider

I suffered from multiple sclerosis (MS). I don't anymore. The paralyzing disease affecting the nervous system has left me. It won't come back. I know that now. I have Tally My Chex—Checkers, I call him—to thank for what seems like a miraculous cure.

The story begins in California, where I worked as a horse trainer and gave riding lessons on a boarding ranch. Even before Checkers was born in 1972, the syndicated owners, sponsored by the Purina Chex Company, had big plans for him. He might make them millions because he was the direct offspring down the line from the royal family who created the quarter-horse registry, known as the Blue-Smoke horses. His great-great-grandfather was called The Traveler, his son was the famous King, and Checkers's daddy was King Fritz. But Checkers was born without testicles. He wouldn't father anyone.

When God doesn't give us a way to do one thing, I think he gives us something else. That something extra for Checkers is his superior intelligence. All horses are intuitive and telepathic. Checkers is tuned in, quick to get what you want him to do, and co-creating with you spontaneously. He is ready to be your partner, but not to be simply ordered around. He responds when invited to participate and he contributes with high performance.

Checkers was two years old when I met him at Tally Ho Farms in Fountain Valley, California. The owners had decided to make a show horse out of him so they could recoup some of their investment. My job was to train him to achieve that goal. The horse and I became attached to each other right away. Checkers was a combination of power and beauty, dark bay in color, sixteen hands, a heavyweight with perfect conformation expected of a champion, with a star on his forehead, a stripe down his nose, and a snip on his muzzle that signaled the innocent mischief he was full of—in case you missed the deep expression in his eyes that revealed his roots back to the old man, King.

Standing on the lower rail of his pipe corral, I leaned over to scratch behind Checkers's ears. In a split-second plunge with his head to my feet, he untied both laces on my tennis shoes. He was known to take things out of the back pockets of anyone's jeans who turned his back on him. I watched Checkers pick up with his teeth a rake that had been left on the inside of his corral. He carried it to the other side and tossed it over the rails.

Before I met him, Checkers had been pushed too hard too soon by an inexperienced trainer. Checkers had blown up at him. Checkers wasn't in the mood to be ridden or asked to perform commanded signals. He was upset with people, but he used his sense of humor to show me who he was and how smart he was and how he wanted to be treated. So I took a different approach. I took the saddle and bridle off and agreed not to train. We agreed to play.

I put Checkers in a round corral. I'd run around the outside and skid my feet down in the dirt and hollar, "Ho!" Checkers was just delighted to follow me. I trotted and walked and turned and did quick rollbacks. He imitated the crazy human outside his corral. After a week or so of this, he was in the mood again and looked forward to my coming to get him. It was a natural step to ride again. He flowed through the cues like a dancer.

Checkers loved the children who visited the stables, and he showed a lot of compassion for baby animals and birds, too. Once he spent a whole month sharing his stall with a mother hen and her chicks without harm to any of them. The chicks would gather around his feet, pecking at grain spilling from his mouth when he ate. He would stand as still as granite to keep from stepping on them. He would be a victim of his compassion after nuzzling a mare next to him who had strangles; from her he would contract pneumonia for a second time in his young life.

The vet had done all he could with antibiotics. He said it was up to Checkers to recover. I stayed the night, spoonfeeding him water because he was too weak and stiff to get it for himself. He began to come around and to flourish soon after. His remaining owner, Mr. Perry, who also owned Tally-Ho Farms, credited me with saving Checkers's life. Checkers and I somehow had bonded our spirits. Our friendship would last well over twenty years. But first I had a responsibility to complete. I continued to train Checkers so that others would be able to ride him and eventually own him. My heart was breaking. I knew I could never come up with the kind of money he was to sell for.

The sad day came, and off he went. After some weeks I went to where he was to visit. Then I tried to face the reality and accept that I'd never see Checkers again. He was being tried out by a wealthy man's daughter to be her show horse.

A few weeks later, as I arrived for work, Mr. Perry asked me to check the automatic waterer in stall 19. I protested, not knowing anything about plumbing, and scoffed, "Why would I want to do that?"

"Just go down there and check if it's working."

I arrived at stall 19, staring at the huge dark hindquarters of a horse that could only be of a King heritage.

"Checkers?" He turned around and put his head on my chest. I just stood there crying, speechless. I looked back down the aisle of stalls and saw my boss with a kerchief, wiping away at his eyes.

"I have to sell this place," he said. "I'm ill. You can have Checkers for the price of his breeding fee, $1,600—if you still want him." This was unheard of because, just from his bloodline alone, he would bring $10,000 to $20,000.

"Sold!" I shouted.

I designed and had a contractor build a home in the Tustin Hills of California. My husband and I sold this place in order to create the down payment needed for a country property where I could have Checkers at home and teach and train there. I also acquired a free lesson-horse to use; she became pals with Checkers.

A dysfunctional marriage cannot be saved by buying a dream home. We soon divorced. I was drawn to Arizona, so I picked up and moved with the horses, my son, and a dog and a cat. Within another year or so I married my next alcoholic—the same partner, just a different face and name.

Body and spirit soon gave out. I manifested multiple sclerosis. I was still riding, working as a real estate agent, and dabbling in songwriting. By this time, Checkers and I were on a visualizing basis for riding cues. I would just picture in my head what I wanted him to do and he would do it.

We were like one in movement together. As a kid in Northern California, I was taught by a Native American to ride with no saddle or bridle. It's an art I have passed on to my students over twenty-eight years. When MS weakened my muscles and my ability to stay balanced, this method of riding made it possible for me to continue to ride Checkers.

On really bad days, I would tie a rope between the garage at the house out to his corral and pull myself out there to feed and groom him. He would welcome me with soft muzzle kisses on my face and arms. He would prop me up by shifting his weight while I was grooming him. I could simply ask Checkers to put his head down, and he would open his mouth and fit the bridle between his own teeth for me.

The multiple sclerosis came and went during the first few years. Doctors hesitated to give a diagnosis, my alcoholic husband offered no support at all, and friends would say, "But you look so well." If I hadn't had Checkers's loving support, I would have gone under. I was about thirty-eight when the condition began. By forty-one I was going downhill in the grip of rapidly progressing MS. By this time, a doctor to told me to get my things in order, that MS could kill me within six to eight weeks. I decided to ride Checkers instead.

I could no longer walk well. My left side felt numb and mostly paralyzed. My speech came out jerkily and sometimes not at all. I was extremely weak and fatigued. I would fall without warning. My vision was blurred. At times I would black out. I had to leave working, to stay at home and try to heal. During his alcoholic rages, my husband would threaten to kill the horses. I would have to learn to live my life with the spirit of the horse to survive and be there to take care of Checkers and the other animals, Missy Starr, a mare, Harley, a German shepherd, and Alexander, a cat.

The unconditional love and support given me by Checkers and the others sustained me long enough to begin to recover and then to reverse the illness. I divorced my husband.

Eventually I had to sell my home, as I could not earn enough money to pay the mortgage. Though I grew stronger as I healed, it was not in time to save the house. A job offer came up in California to direct a charity foundation at home and get paid enough to support all of us, so I moved there after my house sold in Arizona. Shortly after we moved to California, the job fell through, the money ran out, we were homeless—and I was terrified.

I would not give up Checkers. He and the other animals were my only medicine, my only support. With a miracle, I managed to get us all back home in Arizona. We were separated for a month before I was able to begin working again to support us.

The MS was gone. It couldn't compete with the desire to share my life with Checkers. This is not a normal course for multiple sclerosis: It always progresses quickly or slowly to a worsening place.

Checkers is twenty-three years old now. He suffers from carpal arthritis in his left front knee and, I suspect, in his back as well. His eyes looked tired, but they spark up when he sees me coming. His spirit is still working for him. I live in a rented bunkhouse on the Sonoran Desert. We are all together still. I hope my love for Checkers can help him to be free of pain. I hope to be able to provide a beautiful pasture for him to retire in. We don't saddle up anymore, but we ride through every cloud with angels and as far as the stars.

Julie Alex-Rider lives in Cave Creek. She recently started her own real estate company, specializing in conservation-sensitive residential development. She writes and performs her own songs. You can bet she gives Checkers the best care she can provide. She welcomes mail to Box 4650, Cave Creek, Arizona 85331.

Control

The archaeologist showed slides of rock art in caves in what today are called France and Spain. We saw the fabulous, flickering, multi-legged deer and buffalo of Lascaux that everyone who comes from what we call western civilization should know in his genes. We also saw outlines of hands. Anne Duffield, a rock art specialist from California, surmised that some early human blew ochre through a tube, painting his hands and leaving a void where the fingers spread, in an early graffito. What produces more surmise is why some fingertips are missing in some of the pictures.

Duffield likened the purposeful clipping of fingertips to the practice of boxing of feet the Chinese effected before they lost control at Tiananmen Square and perfected the machine gun. You couldn't always keep 'em barefoot and pregnant, but you could fix their feet so they couldn't run away. Later, reflecting on what she'd said, Duffield made her point come home: "These people were moved to sacrifice what must be very important to all humans (hands and feet) because *something*—grief? status?—means that much to them to do it."

What, human mutilation? Surely not!

Surely so. Hohokam babies during one period were bound in their papoose boxes so that the backs of their soft heads deformed, producing an unnatural plane. Aztecs went further, sometimes shaping babies' heads into cones. With a head moulded like that as a child, you could go through life without much worry about your dunce cap falling off.

We need not look so far back into human development as those creative hand silhouettes, some estimated at 33,000 years. We can find examples of human mutilation even in the nineteenth century, when eunuchs still served the Chinese emperor. How do you keep a man subservient, docile, and in no danger of touching your women? A little snicker-snack (a Lewis Carroll term from "Jabberwocky") of the knife does it.

In our enlightened modern era we don't deform humans much anymore—except to symbolically trim the hair of our military men and to alter the faces of our rich women with plastic surgery. We can't entirely give up the practice, though; we're now working on our animal servants.

Somehow a dog as born isn't good enough. We must snip off most of his tail. Or we must box his ears, which means a little unnatural surgery to keep those ears erect. We declaw cats to save the furniture. To control reproductive urges in our pets we crush or cut off—snicker-snack—hormone-producing organs. Let Roman Catholic priests fight the urge: they're intelligent; they understand. Dogs just hump anything and can't be expected to abstain from what Nature has given them. So we upgrade Nature. The dogs and cats, after the initial pain, don't seem to mind. They never blame us. They grow a little chunky, but their behavior becomes more socially acceptable. They weren't going to paint any Picasso-like pictures, anyway, so what's lost? We've done the right thing for population control.

You can't have cats and dogs reproducing ad infinitum, which they'd do if unspayed and unneutered. They're good at that. We already have too many dogs and cats and not enough Vietnamese restaurants. We need to control the animals, just as the relatives of Heloise needed to control Abelard with a little snicker-snack.

A magnificent horse lives just down the hill from our house. Two years old, he is the son of an endurance racer named Eleganté, who also lives down the hill. The young horse stands taller than my head, his chestnut coat shiny and well cared for. Last week a veterinarian came by and—snicker-snack—lightened the load of that magnificent horse by less than a pound. (I wonder what the cutters do with them today. In the wild west of yesteryear, they threw them in a pile and then fried them and called them mountain oysters. And euphemised the act with the verb *to geld*.)

The owner led the beautiful horse out of his pen and explained to me what had happened to him. With my inexperience in horse things I could not have told. Now I know I will not hear unexplained whinnying on moonlit midnights anymore, nor hooves banging on feed barrels and corral slats. The horse has been cut down to human size. He can concentrate his juices on racing; mares will become a memory that no longer disturbs. Something inside me, though, sobs for that horse and for what he doesn't even know he has lost. He never knew the wilderness where his kind originated. And likely he never knew what mares were for.

Maybe that's what I need to keep my lecherous mind on the track. Who would be a better candidate for castration than a man who has suffered three wives and produced two children? Just a little snicker-snack would do it.

Packrat chronicles

Dealing with packrats

The eleven-year-old home I moved into in May 1987 came with a new water heater. It also came with an old Maytag washing machine that perhaps had been handed down for two or three generations, a family heirloom that someone neglected to take with him when he sold the house. A pity. That old washer still surges with life. I found out why.

One day in August when I popped in a load of grungy clothing, closed the top, and pulled out the timer to start the machine, water poured in as usual. As usual, I went inside to escape the heat and continue housework. In about ten minutes I noticed the silence. Usually I can hear the machine sloshing about as it does its dirty job. I heard nothing. I went outside. The tub stood full of tepid water. Nothing moved. I pulled out the timer knob and tried a different location, thinking the timer contacts might have worn. Nothing. That nasty smell of ozone which exudes from electric apparatus told me something was wrong inside.

In no time I had siphoned off the water, pulled out the wet, soapy, but unwashed clothes and dumped them in the kitchen sink, and now I tore into the secrets of the old Maytag. Those washers last so long and run so well without fixing because they are so simple: two belts run from an electric motor, one to the churner, one to a pump. The pump runs continuously but only sends water out when the timer opens a valve, as if to say, "Now!"

Figuring the electric motor must have perished from a fatal overload, I set about removing it with my tools. Sure enough, when I'd isolated the motor and touched life-giving electricity to its two wires, it failed to move. It did smoke a bit, as if to ask for quick burial in the dump. I called around. A new one would cost about $90. I drove into town to buy a new heart for the washer. I installed it. As I sweated under the upturned machine, I saw little black grains of rice on the concrete slab under the machine. Then I saw the hair and twigs. Some sort of rodent had tried to build a nest behind the white panels. Packrats, I guessed. They'd come through a port in the back where the exhaust hose exited. With flattened beer cans and self-tapping screws, I plugged up the hole, tested the machine, and went back, I thought, into the twice-a-week laundry business.

For a day. On my next load, I smelled the ozone before I noticed the machine wasn't running. I yanked the cord from the wall, but I was too late. Just as the human brain dies in about three minutes when deprived of oxygen, the heart of a Maytag bites the dust, I found, when certain wires cross without benefit of insulation. Angered, I tore into the machine again. The trouble must be in the timer or the wiring, I diagnosed, and opened up the top.

Native Arizonans know and visitors learn that packrats love the plastic insulation on electrical wires. Park a car in the desert, leave the hood up, goes the advice. Otherwise, the rats will build a nest on your engine, throw a dinner party, and use your car's ignition wires as hors d'oeuvres. Inside the cable run I found bare wires, inexpertly gnawed. When the timer was pulled on, confusing signals had been sent to the motor until it quickly gave up its $90 ghost. Another trip into town, it would mean. More sealant to keep out the pests. Then I took the rich man's way out. I called a Maytag repairman. He sounded busy, not like the ones in the television commercials. Yes, he could come out tomorrow and would bring a new motor and would guarantee it for 90 days. I said nothing about packrats.

Like a surgeon repairing tiny blood vessels or isolating nerves, I carefully taped the chewed wiring, put the top back, and awaited the serviceman. He came about noon, as the sun scorched the side of the house where the laundry lives. He squatted in the little outdoor room, sweating and manipulating his tools until the new motor whirred without a cough. He ran through a wash cycle while sipping ice water. The machine worked like new, he said, and I guessed that it did.

That night as I sat at the kitchen table reading, something at the kitchen sink six feet away caught my peripheral vision. I turned my head. A small rat, with light brown back and whitish underside, stepped out from under the sink and stood looking at me. Thinking fast, I grabbed a chunk of quartz from the table and threw it at the rat. The rock missed by six inches and dented the cabinet under the sink. The rat slipped back under the sink without a word.

The next day, while stopping at the local printing office, I asked Naturewise Eleanor Radke what to use in a rat trap. It was a mistake.

"I hope you mean a live trap," she said, emphasizing *live*. No, I said, I didn't mean live, I mean dead, and went on to explain the problems, including $150 in resuscitating an otherwise good washing machine.

Eleanor is nice even if she doesn't agree with you. "Well, I suppose you could give the packrats what they seem to like best, insulation from electrical wiring." I imagined making a paste of such plastic and a firm cheese, and squeezing it into the trigger on a hefty trap. That is what I did. That night I never awoke when the trap snapped out the life of the old male when he tried to enter my kitchen again. In the morning, there he lay. I tossed his stiff body out on the deck, an example to the others to take off.

They didn't learn. Now each night I could hear them working under the house. They scratched. They ran. They explored. It sounded at times as if they grawed at the concrete block walls as a way of merely flossing their teeth.

I set the killer trap again, this time under the house, in a crawl space they'd entered by tunneling, following the sewer line in from the drain field. To plug up their entrance, I poured sand down their burrow, followed by a flushing of water. When that failed, I tried a gallon of bleach down the hole. They worked around it. I piled on rocks. The animals squirmed through. They ignored the trap. It remains dusty and bloodless, the bait long turned to dust, the trigger still cocked, waiting for the next curious rodent.

Hearing a home fix-up artist on radio describing how to cure a slow sewer line problem by looking for wasp nests in the soil stack—the vent pipe that comes up through the roof—I decided to solve my other problem by looking down the pipe. Up on the roof I went with ladder and flashlight. Squinting, I could look far down the pipe. No wasp nests clogged it. But at the bottom a familiar rodent face looked up at me. He seemed to be smiling.

From then on it was war. I bought D-Con rat poison, the kind that comes in a waxed box you tear open for the rats to get at the poisoned rice inside. Dutifully, I crawled under the house and placed the poison. A week later it sat untouched. But the rats had been busy. In one exploration under the house, when I shone my flashlight into a far corner, I saw a touching family scene: A large rat licked at four half-size rats, obviously her children. She looked up when I flashed the light, but did not disappear until I crawled closer. Then the family split and melted into the concrete blocks by climbing over them and into their hollow centers.

While under the house, I noticed other damage done by the rats. They'd stripped all the pink fiberglass insulation they could reach from around the edges of the house. It made excellent nesting material, if a little itchy. The doorbell had stopped working. I found out why when I saw the insulation removed from the cable: Two separate wires had become one.

The doorbell must have buzzed for hours until it finally burned out. At least the shorted buzzer hadn't started a fire under the house, perhaps because it carried only twenty-four volts. The rats somehow knew not to mess with 110.

Now I carried 2x4s under the house. Sweating and coughing in the glassy dust, I nailed them to the foundation sills over the concrete blocks. Trapped, the rats could not get out. Or so I thought. At night I could hear their desperate gnawing. It went on for three days. Then the sounds diminished. Still, one rat, at least, must have been at large.

On my next trip under the house I dragged in a tub of concrete and a trowel. With difficulty, I plastered up the hole where the sewer pipe penetrated the concrete blocks. I brought in a can of plastic foam and filled in holes under the sink where the old man rat must have chewed his way into my kitchen. I left more boxes of D-Con.

At last silence told me the rats had departed, one way or another. And it wasn't as if I'd spread poisons into the environment. The poisoned rice and the rats that ate it remain entombed under the house. It is cool and silent there now. Nothing moves. Nothing had better. My daughter Lizz, the environmentalist, hates me for what I did, but I don't mind.

Some of the best people in this world have killed rats and walked away from shame.

The packrat scourge

Leslie Evans (not his real name) hated packrats. Everyone in Cave Creek and Carefree knew it. No one knew why, but the hatred simmered as an accepted trait just under Leslie's sandy-gray hair and pale blue eyes. Residents would point out Leslie to their winter vistors and whisper, "He's the man who hates packrats." Sometimes the visitors asked, "Well, why not? Who do you know who loves packrats?" They soon forgot about Leslie as a hot topic.

 Leslie is gone now, but he owned almost five acres up on the east side of Black Mountain, and he lived alone in a house stuffed in among the boulders. He made a monthly tour of his land to look for encroachments—and any signs of packrat activity.

 Leslie had fought in the Korean War. He left two toes there but brought back a love of flame throwers. Whenever Leslie came upon a packrat nest, he brought in his military surplus big gun and soon there was no packrat nest. He never saw a packrat, but that didn't matter. He loved zapping the pile of cactus sherds and bark and seeing the black cloud that soared as if a miniature atom bomb had gone up. Neighbors got used to the roar of the jellied gasoline, the *whomp!* as it hit, and the black cloud rising. The sounds and sights weren't that much different from those made by propane-fired balloons that floated over the foothills in winter months. Luck was with him; the fires never spread.

After one of his monthly sorties on the slopes to find and destroy the enemy, Leslie came back sweaty and dirty. He set his flame thrower down in the garage, then realized he should have parked his pickup truck in the shade. When he tried to start it, nothing happened. When he lifted the hood—well, you know the rest.

Leslie became so enraged he fired away with his flame thrower. When Rural Metro arrived, the fire crew knew what had happened. They tried to stifle grins, and when they couldn't, they put on smoke masks so as not to embarrass Leslie; he was, after all, a customer.

"Probably best not to mention this to your insurance company," said the fire crew's leader. "My brother-in-law rebuilds engines, if you're interested."

Packrat wars

On this thanksgiving day of 1990, perhaps I should be thankful that an intelligence greater than man's has been proven to exist.

He and I have been at it for two weeks now. I wish for his death, or, if that is too extreme, for him to pack up his rubble and take it out where he came from, the desert. He lives now in a labyrinth of his making in fiberglass insulation I wrapped around the giant water heater at the house. It's a logical site for a packrat, warm, certainly. Dry, as it's sheltered under a roof. And, as the intelligent animal knows, hard for human hands or coyotes or big snakes to get at.

If he'd been a little less habitual about it I could have tolerated him. He had to bring to his new home all the detritus he'd use in a rock crevice or under a cactus in the desert. My home is an oasis in the desert. He chose me. He chose to bring staghorn cholla balls that put spines in my feet, right through my shoes, that tangle with the laundry nearby. He doesn't deposit his feces in the garden, where they might do some good, but litters the back of the washing machine and his water heater home with them.

While I have never seen this packrat, I know plenty about him. He may be smarter than me. In the first battles of our war, he has won, and I respect him for that. I baited a rat trap with peanut butter, a thick, nutty kind that sticks to the roof of the mouth, and, I hoped, to the trigger on the trap. (Yes, my darling daughter, this is a vicious, back-breaking snapper of a trap, not a live trap.) The next morning I came out to remove the stiff gray body from the trap. What I found was a snapped trap. Not only was the peanut butter gone, but the stiff wire that links the killer bar to the trigger had been wrested from its home. Presumably the rat had added it to his nest. The trap would no longer work.

So I brought in a new trap. My experience with the traps is so great now that I can bait and set them blindfolded without getting a finger snapped. This time, though, I trained my rat, I told myself. For two nights I put out the new trap with the killer bar unset. The rat could feast without fear and grow comfortable with the machine of his coming destruction. Then he was ready.

The peanut butter went down. The trap moved gingerly onto the ground in the few inches littered with spines between washing machine and water heater. The rat's hour was at hand, or so I thought.

The next morning I found the trap still set. The peanut paste had been carefully removed from the trigger. That dangerous bar had not only been licked clean; tiny teeth had scraped off even the oil. The trigger glowed bright and coppery again.

We are not dealing with an ordinary rat here, I realized. This one probably steals electricity to watch television on a tiny set he has scrounged. He may have hooked up a modem to my phone lines; I've heard a certain scratchiness in my ear lately that is not AT&T trying to sabotage my MCI connection.

Now I'm experimenting with a piece of aluminum screen that wraps around the trigger. Wired in place, the screen's job is to keep the bait secure. To get to the peanut butter, my rat will really have to pump iron on that trigger. And that will do it. Or it will inspire the beady-eyed one to outrat me again. In the meantime, don't expect me to sign a petition outlawing leg-hold traps in Arizona. And now you know why we ate traditional turkey at our home this thanksgiving.

Packrat lifestyles

You never see us if we can help it,
 and if you do, we're in trouble.
Daytime's for sleeping. We can't see in sun,
 but in dimness of our rubble.

Like you, we enjoy both good nights and bad,
 while chomping cactus carefully,
To leave the spines, points up, for you to touch,
 to step on, curse us darefully.

Like you, we celebrate the solstices
 and ev'ry trinket we gather.
We don't yowl about it like Coyote;
 a lower profile we'd rather.

Like you, we celebrate coming of age
 with revels lasting many nights.
But you, Biped, will never learn of our
 unsqueakable puberty rites.

To trap a rat

Hearing of my cruel attempts to discourage
Neotoma (*Packraticus americanus*) from living
near my home, my animal-rights daughter
Lizz sent a live or harmless trap at
Christmas. Unfortunately, it was intended for

mice, and not just any mouse. The blue plastic box, bent in its middle, would accommodate any small rodent who was not claustrophobic. The concept was simple: The mouse, sensing peanut butter at the end of the plastic tunnel, would crawl in. When its weight passed the middle, the tube would tilt, and a door would slam close and lock. The people who make the trap, Trap-Ease Rodent Traps of Santa Ana, California, considered even the squeamish: "Sanitary—You never need to see or touch the rodent."

Lizz, realizing the trap was too small for the giant packrats which inhabit the Sonoran desert, soon sent another, slightly larger one. I smeared peanut butter inside and set the trap by the washing machine, out back of the house, as they say in Australia. In the first week I caught and released a lawyer, a building inspector, and two bible salesmen, but no *Neotomae*.

Packrat solutions

When I first came to the foothills I quickly learned about a major nemesis of which Easterners know nothing: packrats. In the local paper we newcomers were warned to leave our hoods up to discourage the nasty rodents from building nests on top our cars' engines. One of the packrat's greatest culinary delights, I learned in amazement, was automotive ignition wire insulation. Put peanut butter in mouse traps, if you will; use plastic insulation for packrats, I was told.

Jim Hill of Blue Bird Books offered his recipe for keeping the little pests away from car wiring. "I'm not sure it will work," he said in his self-effacing way, "but it sounds as if it might." Jim's solution: the super-hot juice squeezed from jalapeño peppers. Coat that on your car's wires and forget about packrats.

I remembered Jim's cure three years later when I cleaned out a shed at the new ranch. The shed would make an ideal parking place for our pickup truck. The trouble was that packrats had nested in the shed under an old engine block that lay in the sand. I cleaned out their mess of mostly dead cactus parts. Not a rat showed himself.

The next morning, though, the spare tire, locked under the truck bed, was missing. The lock remained in place. Not only that, but one tire sat squished and flat on the ground. (Months later I found the missing wheel under a mesquite tree fifty feet away where the packrats had somehow moved it to become part of the debris of their new nest.)

Rather than leave the truck's hood up, where an errant eagle might built a nest, I tried Jim Hill's advice. First I bought a packet of Mad Coyote chili powder, made right here in Cave Creek. I stirred it into about three ounces of olive oil until the consistency of latex paint dripped off my paint brush. Then I spent twenty minutes carefully coating the truck's wires and hoses. It was worth the effort, I figured, slamming the hood down as if daring the beasts to have a bite.

When I returned at sunset to check out the truck, a faint sound of mariachi music floated along the drive to meet me. Perhaps I'd left the radio on. It was not the radio, I learned upon hoisting the hood. About thirty packrats, chewing all the while, looked up at me. Some wore tiny serapes and hats one sees south of our border. A trio, perched on the air-conditioning condenser, played mariachi music. The spark plug wires lay silver and bare. One of the pack rats let out a belch and kept on chewing, oblivious of one as stupid as me.

Over a beer at the Blue Bird, Jim Hill consoled me. In his five years out here in Arizona, Jim now has learned about a subspecies called Mexican packrat.

"I didn't promise the jalapeño sauce trick would work," he gently chided. Now we know it does not.

To soar with eagles

One of the first things I did on moving to the desert was to subscribe to the local paper. I figured it would help me fit in, would give me some local knowledge helpful for navigating new channels. I was partly right. But one of the paper's freelance Nature writers suggested leaving your car's hood up. That ploy would prevent an infestation of packrats in your car's engine compartment, he said. So I left the hood up. The idea apparently was correct, because I haven't seen any packrats, and I've not had to replace any spark plug wires that the rats reportedly like for breakfast.
    Unfortunately, though, the raised hood served as some kind of signal for a bald eagle family. Before I knew it, they'd built a nest on top the engine. Before I could remove the nest, a park ranger saw it and ordered a barbed-wire fence built around my car. The eagles and their eaglet are doing fine, thank you, but it will be another two months, Smokey tells me, before I can approach the car. I can't imagine what the groceries in the back seat will smell like then. I hope they haven't attracted any packrats.

In the meantime, I'm working on a campaign to decertify the bald eagle as this country's national bird. They're really rather smelly creatures, I've found. How about substituting the English sparrow? Or the turkey buzzard?

Is this really desert?

A Wisconsin visitor in early May looked at the greenery through our truck windshield as we bounced across back-country Carefree and innocently asked, "Is this really desert?"

Hard to believe, I explained, but, yes, Virginia, this is real desert. Geographically or botanically, the proper term is Sonoran desert, characterized by more rainfall—ten inches each year, on average—than the sandy, stereotypical deserts of Hollywood, but still arid. We have here a semi-green band of plant life reaching from earth to rarely more than ten feet into the sky, mostly low shrubs, some trees, including mesquite, ironwood, and a usually-leafless one called palo verde.

This greenery supports a variety of life, including some forty year-around species of birds (115 with transients), mountain lion, mule deer, javelina (or collared peccary), and plenty of insects. We're famous for rattlesnakes—although in five years here I've seen only two live ones—scorpions (three killed in the house last year), and spiders: black widow, tarantula, and the nasty brown recluse, whose bite is so toxic that, if you recover, you need plastic surgery to cover up where skin will never grow back. Pleasant place. (I didn't know then that tarantulas are mellow—and virtually atoxic.)

The hallmark of our Sonoran desert is the saguaro cactus, that green traffic cop with sometimes more than two arms. It can top sixty feet in height, can weigh tons when swollen with August monsoon rains, and seems to possess intelligence. Anecdotes about *Carnegiea gigantea,* a cereus, tell of it crashing to earth, squashing whatever gets in its way, as if it had taken lessons from lumbering beasts back in the dinosaur era.

Like the entire Sonoran desert, the saguaro's future is threatened, not only by the creators of Disney desert but by the lowly pack rat, *Neotoma*. Bert Edises, a retired lawyer, writing for the conservation committee of the Cave Creek Improvement Association, in an article published in a distant back issue of the *Sentinel*, indicts *Neotoma*:

"Rodents—and the packrat in particular—are blamed for the failure of attempts to propagate saguaros from seedlings," Bert says. He notes a test, in which 800 seedlings left in unfenced plots had only fourteen still alive after six months. "In another year and a half those fourteen were dead, as were 770 seedlings from a second planting of 800. The work of destruction was attributed to packrats—half of whose annual diet is provided by cacti, including the prominent saguaro."

Guess I'd rather be suddenly squashed by a saguaro than nibbled out of my mind over months by *Neotoma*. When Geoffrey Platts tries to make me feel guilty for zapping packrats, I tell him that a saguaro made me do it.

Snakes alive

Be kind to your no-footed friends,
For that snake may be somebody's mother...

Snakes of the Arizona highways

Before the great semiannual Kiwanis clean-up of our roadsides, I want to get out in the sun some morning and enlarge my snake collection. The intent is to mount the critters on a piece of plywood, with suitable captions for each. Here are some of the species I expect to collect:

Stereo Tape Snake Distantly related to the tapeworm. Usually rust brown and one-quarter-inch wide, but may be half-inch in some affluent locales. Appears in loose coils. Extremely dangerous. May emit loud noises when used in a tape player. Handle with gloves and wear earphones.

Fan Belt Snake Observed in many varieties and sizes, but generally black or gray. Often seen with tail in mouth in loop mode. Cloth-like scales.

Rope Snake May resemble nylon, hemp, manila, or cotton rope, braided or stranded, often with cow's tail.

Cable Snake Related to rope snake, but usually does not coil readily. May be metallic colored or covered with a plastic-like film. Dangerous to domestic animals.

Casing Snake Often marked with letters that resemble such names and logos as

Goodyear, General. Prefers open highway to roadside.

Rigger's Snake Usually presents a hook at one end. May be dull black or, in springtime, covered with scales the texture of woven nylon with colorful patterning. Sometimes hooks appear at both ends, usually during mating season, in August.

One-Eyed Snake (Moulted skin only; the snake is rarely seen.) Found mostly along lovers' lanes and at drive-in movie theaters. Though heavily crushed by tires when found, usually some life remains. Cream to gray in color. Stretchy. Caution: Suspected carrier of social diseases.

Visit from a freckled beauty

Early one morning I bounded up to my office. As I hit the bottom step, I stopped. Something lay across my path. It was cylindrical, about three feet long, with a viper-like head. First I saw the rattles. That stopped me. I did not jump back, remembering Geoffrey Platts's lessons on how to communicate goodwill to a snake. I was not frightened at all, nor did my heart beat faster. I looked on this encounter as an opportunity to visit with a denizen of the desert rarely seen in daylight. The western diamondback rattler works at night, sensing infrared radiation from living things warmer than the Earth. What this one was doing in bright sunshine I could not imagine, but I took the opportunity to get a close look. I stopped, wished the snake good morning, and bent closer to see the details. The snake slowly moved down the step and I moved back, quickly into the house, not to get away but to call Jane and Mark to see this patterned footless wonder.

With six eyes looking at it, the snake slipped purposefully for the garden at the south end of the house, moving along the bricks, looking for something. At no time did it coil, hiss, or rattle. When the snake disappeared from view, we went in the house. In a few minutes I heard Mark go out the front door, and then say something muffled but loud as he shut the door hard. The snake was walking by the door, he reported. Jane shrieked.

"Use the back door," I suggested. Mark did.

Later, I said to Jane by way of provocation, "It's the snake again. He wants to come in. Says it's too hot out there. Okay?"

Visit from a rattler

It was early in the morning. I came out the front door and there he was, yellow and brown, coiled like a mooring line on a metate not eight feet away. Of course I called Jane and Mark, and they came out to look. He didn't move a muscle except to flick his infrared heat sensor out from between his nostrils. It was September, maybe moulting time, and maybe he couldn't see too well through last year's skin. So he tried to figure out what these big heat sinks were standing around. We talked gently to him, telling him how beautiful he was. Uncoiled, he might be three feet long, four if you were scared. He looked too small around the middle to handle a packrat, but he could sure gulp down some mice.

    The old Maytag washer sat on the front porch doing temporary duty until Kaysen came around to fix the more modern Whirlpool out back. The metate sat behind the washer. The exhaust hose from the washer squirted gray water at a wall of the house, where it splattered and then ran down the steps onto the driveway. I figured the snake came there either for the moisture or to wait for lunch in the form of some bird or animal that came to drink. We wanted to make him feel welcome, but we weren't about to invite him into the house for breakfast, even if we did have mice.

Each time one of us came outside, we'd look to see if he was still there. As the sun came around the house in the afternoon, he moved in under the metate as best he could, in the shade, coils gripping the damp bricks. Because he couldn't close those eyes, he stuck his heart-shaped head under his coils. No rampaging washing machine nor weird two-legged animals were going to bother him. It was sunshiny, time for sleeping.

We did notice his tail. At the end were about six rattles followed upstream by about four inches of black, no black and white bands as we'd seen on a western diamondback rattlesnake on our back steps just two days before. Our new snake was not a coontail. We weren't sure what he was. Maybe he was a she. (Just as people call boats *she,* they seem to call snakes *he.* Why is that?)

At dusk the snake stretched out and moved slowly off the porch—for his nightly hunt, we assumed. The next day he was back under the metate. Kaysen's crew came to service the washers. I dragged the Maytag about eight feet away, carefully plugged in an extension cord, and warned the men about the snake, but he didn't bother them. It was daytime and he was sleepy. That night we saw him slip away again.

After dark it began to rain. The snake sat coiled on a corner of a stone-walled planter. He seemed to be enjoying the moisture, such as it is in Arizona: more of a drizzle. In the morning, he was back under the metate, head tucked under his coils, fast asleep.

At lunch at the Blue Bird Cafe, we told botanist Steve Jones about the snake, and tried to describe him.

"Green or greenish tint?"

"I think so. Black tail."

"Might be a Mohave. Forty times as toxic as other rattlers. But not any meaner or provokable."

We gulped. Steve and family followed us back to the porch to see our little friend.

"That's a black-tailed rattler," Steve said. "Probably the most mild-mannered, best-behaved of the rattlesnakes. I knew as soon as I saw his head. See those slanted lines going through his eyes?"

We bade the Joneses goodbye and kissed the snake goodnight. Maybe it was too much to expect of a wild beast, too much gawking and talking. In the morning, the snake was gone. It had been a wonderful if gingerly three days and nights, a chance to observe a beauty close up that most people never see alive.

Later, when telling Geoffrey Platts about our visit, he congratulated us on our good fortune. "Usually a snake won't stay that long," he said.

We wonder now, days afterwards, what message the snake brought for us, what he was supposed to mean, for such collisions of man and snake are no more accidental than the rest of life. Maybe the meeting was so that we could bring you this story, and, through these words you could appreciate a snake you've never seen.

Rattlesnake rentals

My entrepreneurial spirit, breathed into me by my father when I was about twelve, appears now and then like a genie. Mostly, my ideas about good businesses flow forth for others, not for myself. That's only fair.

For our nation's 200th anniversary, I undertook to republish Ben Franklin's *Pennsylvania Gazette* of 1776 for sale to schools. The concept failed, bringing my company financial loss but helping the beleauguered optometric industry; all that small type was daunting, especially with *f*s masquerading for *s*es.

That is why I hestitate—for a moment—before foisting this idea on Geoffrey Platts, who seems to have time to pioneer new ideas, to turn them into fresh capital. It is a simple concept, requiring only a bit of local advertising and publicity to make it go: the rental of rattlesnakes.

You may scoff. Who would want to rent a venomous creature with no legs? And therein lies the market.

(Keep this close to your chest, Geoffrey. It's a great idea, but don't just give it away. You may be able to license it.)

That market can be defined by this jingle, which could find use in radio and television spots:

People...people who have packrats
  Are the neediest people in the world.
Rattlers...love to eat those packrats,
  And Platts sure has the rattlers for your rats.

Foothills, here's what happened in recent times, if your history got rusty. As the place built up, people drove off the rattlers. Not in their Mercedes-Benzes and Jaguars and Cadillacs, but with their shotguns or the cooperation of Rural Metro in between ambulance runs and firefighting.

When Desert Mountain opened its three green golf courses for its first tournament about 1991, a paid posse of rattlesnake hunters swept the greens. The shooters cleaned the golf courses of more than 100 rattlers, they claimed, making the tournament safe for everything except round missiles called balls.

No more rattlers, plenty more rats. That's a theory of economics or ecology that really works. The rats, finding their chief enemies blasted off their turf, took the opportunity to proliferate.

Packrats rather like people. The rats are nocturnal, so you usually don't see them. They sleep in those monstrous constructions of cactus spines you find in the real desert, usually in the middle of a prickly pear cluster. Not much can get at them there—except for large snakes with expansible mouths.

If the human residents have scraped away the cactus, the rats would rather inhabit their garages, carports, water heaters, or even under the hoods of their trucks and cars, where the exotic taste of wiring insulation adds spice to their diets.

Packrats are so smart they're almost untrappable. I've put out killer traps baited with peanut butter, caviar, jewelry, wire insulation, and head cheese. The traps succeeded, sadly, only in killing a curious cactus wren. (I know, Geoffrey: redundancy; all cactus wrens are curious creatures.)

So the only thing that works besides a flamethrower on the rats' nests are rattlesnakes.

If you can't find any snakes around—and now you know why—you can always (except in winter months) rent those rattlers from Geoffrey. That's if he takes my idea and slithers with it.

(Suggest, Geoffrey, that you charge by the running foot. Good English measure and not subject to fudging. Hey, you could sell venom on the side, guaranteeing that the rattler was milked of its poison before letting it out on hire.)

The old man and the snake
By Barbara Sciacca

The old man stepped to the door and looked out at the morning. The sun had just crept over the rise to the east, and with its very first rays he could catch the promise of the relentless heat that would envelop the day.

He held a coffee cup in his left hand, satisfied that it had cooled a bit, while he let the screen door shut easily with his right.

As he lowered his eyes to ease himself down on the step, an ever-so-slight movement to the left caught his eye. At the same time that he saw the pattern on the ground take shape, his body reacted, even before his thoughts were in gear.

He leaped backward, losing his footing, and came down hard on the top step. The coffee flew from his cup down his shirt front, the moist heat enveloping his chest. The adrenaline rush, the fear, got him first. In the next split second, he felt anger over his stumble, the coffee, and most of all, anger because he had felt the fear.

The object of this mobilized energy had been on its way across the yard to find a cool spot for the day. At least a place out of the sun, a place to rest up for another night of hunting mice and other little animals that had eluded it this time.

As the old man flailed wildly and thudded to the step, the snake quickly gathered itself into itself and took the stance of one getting ready to defend itself. Of course, as it poised itself into this position, and just in case the old man might not have actually noticed it, the snake rattled.

The old man backed up and grabbed a shovel leaning against the porch. As he calmed himself, muttering, "Damn, damn," between clenched teeth, he advanced on the snake. He raised the shovel precisely in front of him as both a shield and a weapon.

"Hey, what are you doing, Old Man?" said the snake.

With this, the old man really backed up suddenly and looked around, the way people do when they absolutely don't trust what appears to be happening.

"I won't strike if you won't strike, okay?" The snake said this quietly. You could hear the desperation in its voice, which sounded as though it was coming from a tin can buried in the ground.

The old man heard it. "Look what you made me do!" he said angrily. "What the hell do you think you're doing here? You'll get the dog or the cat. I just can't have you around here. You'll wind up where I least expect you, and then I won't be prepared, and you'll get me."

"Look," said the pit viper, its body beginning to heat up uncomfortably from the sun, "I just want to go somewhere and cool off and sleep. I don't want your cat or your dog. I've been waiting all night for the packrat in your shed, but I missed it. I'm hungry, but sleep will do."

The old man was sweating. He felt unprepared for this beginning to his day. He was feeling shaky. He backed up to the porch and leaned against it while he tried to sense if he was losing his mind. All the while he watched the snake. It was getting tired, trying hard to look fierce and coiled. It was beginning to waver noticeably. It had stopped rattling except for a twitch here and there.

Someone was going to have to give ground, and, by God! it wasn't going to be the old man. He could not just walk away. The snake was going to have to be dealt with.

Again, the snake stood up. Again, it spoke.

"Old man, this is no contest. We never win with humans if they choose to kill us. But listen, wouldn't it be okay if I just got out of here? Honest, I was just passing through. I'll leave your packrats alone. Okay?"

Snakes can't back up, and this one was afraid to turn its back on the old man. Nevertheless, there was no hole to disappear into, nowhere to burrow until the danger was over. So the snake gradually straightened out, heading away from the old man.

The snake gained a few feet, then turned its head and looked at the man with its right eye. Then it went a few feet further. All this was done in a nonchalant way, no quick movements. Soon it was at the end of the yard, close to the road. It deliberately slid over a rock and out of sight.

All the while, the old man held the shovel poised. As the snake disappeared over the rock, the man slowly lowered the shovel to the ground, exhaled deeply, and stood there. The coffee already had dried on his shirt.

Barbara Sciacca's story first appeared in the *Foothills Sentinel*.

Were it knot for discovering it twice...
By Jim Raymond
Carefree

Walking my faithful dog one day in Carefree, I was disturbed to discover a mutilated common king snake in a brittle bush next to the road. Someone had cut off the small snake's head and tied its body into a tight overhand knot around some of the main branches of the bush. The entire snake appeared badly mangled.

How, I wondered, could anyone be so cruel? I decided it was the thoughtless act of some neighborhood boys who caught and killed the helpless snake and then tied it in the bush. I promised myself to lecture them if I ever caught them doing such a thing. Only four days later I would learn how wrong my conclusion was.

I was walking my dog again, not forty yards from where I found the dead snake four days earlier. I heard a violent commotion in the brush on a small knoll just fifteen yards from where my dog and I stood in the roadway. I couldn't imagine what was making such a disturbance, but suddenly a great horned owl tried to arise from the brush. Wings beating furiously, it seemed tethered to the bushes or caught in a trap. Suddenly it broke free. Clutched in its claws was a heavy, four-foot-long, writhing king snake.

The owl could barely stay aloft with its heavy quarry. It flew about 200 feet before it dropped the snake in the road. Running up to the snake, I was amazed to discover its head torn off, and, although writhing vigorously, the snake was tightly tied into an overhand knot. The owl scolded us from a nearby palo verde. As soon as we walked a short distance away, it flew down, retrieved its prey, and flew away with great effort.

What I had witnessed was a life-and-death struggle—the snake tying itself into the bush in an effort to gain safety and leverage; the owl chomping off its head and pulling it from the bush. I've never spoken to another person who has ever found a knotted snake in a bush or anywhere else, dead or alive, or witnessed such a spectacle. I believe this was a highly unusual episode of our southwest's wild kingdom.

Dog barks with forked tongue
By Mindi Kugler
Carefree

Blaze, our Labrador, was accustomed to barking three times when he wanted in the front door. So when his relentless noise did not subside, I became irritable. With less than an hour in my schedule to finish chores, I was on the run with laden arms from one end of the house to the other. I took exception to Blaze as he interrupted my pace.

Reluctantly, I put down the stack of towels perched on top of sheets and drew back the vertical blinds of our picture window. With a clear side view of the porch, I could see no one standing in front of the screen.

We had just added the screen. In fact, it was so new my husband had not yet installed the deadbolt lock in the upper hole. I was reassured by the thought that the handle on the screen door was locked, as was the deadbolt and handle on the wooden door. If someone was trying to break in, they'd have a hard time of it.

Blaze's barking was more than persistent; it escalated into impatient snapping. My concern grew to anger, as I thought Blaze was sending me a message: "I want in, and it had better be now!"

I unlocked the wooden door and whipped it open with my own boisterous response. At the top of my lungs I yelled, "Blaze!"

I found myself eyeball to eyeball with the largest bull snake I had seen in the twenty-eight years I've been in the foothills. The snake jerked his head back as my hot breath met his nostrils.

With imperceptible reflex, I slammed the door and fastened both locks. Later, I asked myself why I had taken such care to turn the mechanisms. Intellectually, I knew the snake could not enter through a closed door. But my emotions had long since consumed any logical thinking. My focus was on the forked tongue and how quickly it jutted, an image indelibly burned in my mind.

The snake had slithered up the outside of the screen, come through the deadbolt hole, dropped down in the crevice between the two doors, and was raising its head to discover new territory when we met. I grabbed my car keys and the portable phone, then headed out the back door. After confining Blaze, I dialed the fire department.

With a carefully worded objective description, I kept myself calm while giving necessary information. The fire department was on its way. I waited.

The snake grew impatient and began to look for another way out. It discovered a space between the screen and the threshold large enough to squeeze between. I had noted that the diameter at the midpoint of the snake filled the hole drilled for the deadbolt.

As the reptile began to slide the length of its body onto the porch, I backed off considerably and phoned the fire department again. They had received two calls from residents facing rattlesnakes in their yards, so my dilemma took a back seat.

We remained on the line together while I described how the snake was heading for a small opening under the house. As the snake fully retreated to a cooler place, I canceled my call for help.

I pulled the carpenter's measuring tape from the van and extended it to seven feet, covering the length along the house the snake had stretched just before it disappeared.

"It's seven feet long!" I screamed into the receiver. I had forgotten the fire department had hung up when the snake disappeared. I looked around, embarrassed about my display of fear in the face of such little danger. No one was there, anywhere. My heart rate slowed.

Only Blaze, the snake, and I were aware of my panic. And I knew Blaze would never tell.

Snakes in love
By Geoffrey Platts
From TREK! Man Alone in the Arizona Wild, copyright © 1991 by Geoffrey Platts. Used by permission of the author.

I was about to set off again when I heard a light rattle and, to my excitement, spotted a pair of black-tailed rattlesnakes wrapped around each other. Since snakes are chiefly solitary creatures, these two had to be making love! The smaller one, which I took to be the female, had a stunted rattle and she, no doubt piqued at me for having disturbed their loveplay, withdrew to a shady nook 'neath a boulder—with the male pursuing her. I crept slowly to within six feet of them—and then stepped back sharply, for she seemed to make an aggressive lunge and came part way out of the darkened hole. Was she really angry at my having disrupted a moment of rare reptilian rapture? Or was this forward move of hers just curiosity? No matter—this lissom lady was no longer eager to consummate her love with a human voyeur in the vicinity, so she slithered out of the hole, wound her way upwards through a tangle of dead flood-jammed sticks, and vanished into a jumble of boulders on higher ground. As she slid away, the burnished gold diamond markings on her back expanded and contracted in a most fascinating way. The more placid male lingered a while and then with his forked black heat sensor flickering in and out made his departure, though sluggishly.

Earlier this year I was privileged to come across a courting pair of western diamond-back rattlesnakes ("coontails") who were far less concerned with my peeping presence than these two. It's profoundly sad that most humans will kill rattlers on sight. Those humans could learn so much by keeping their distance, staying still, and observing the snakes. Far better to relocate them than to kill. That reverence for life again. Henry David Thoreau put it well:

"Every creature is better alive than dead—men, moose and pine trees—and he who understands it aright will rather preserve its life than destroy it."

Pat Lyon

Arizona animal stories from other authors

The pecking order
By Richard L. Hoover
Carefree

First comes our big Samoyed (looks like a polar bear and weighs about 115 pounds), then the Harris's hawk (the Arizona eagle, with a wingspan of about four feet), followed by the ground squirrel, then the flicker (a woodpecker), the quail, the chipmunk, the dove, the cardinal, the finch, the cactus wren, the sparrow, and finally the hummingbird.

Every so often there show up some javelinas (peccary or Arizona wild pig). They become Number One. Even though we hear the coyotes at night, we don't see them, with the exception of one running across the driveway.

In effect, our property is an animal refuge. We bought this land about twenty-five years ago when it was cheap, so we have a twenty-acre protected plot for our friends, the animals of Arizona.

We feed the birds. The present covey of quail is about the thirtieth generation to consider us friends. When we are in our pool, the quail will walk on the cool decking within about eight feet of us. If we get out of the water, about twenty feet is all the leeway they allow us.

I have learned to communicate with some of these birds. The Harris's hawk makes a sound I can mimic, a shrill whistle through my front upper teeth. It sounds like short bursts of high-pressure steam. Using the same whistle, I can talk to the cardinal by making the whistle sound like *pretty, pretty, pretty.*

When the Harris's hawk lands on the birdbath or the pool fence, all the other birds give way. The big dog just lies there and does nothing. If the hawk is not around, all the remaining birds congregate, but an order of priority is established.

We used to have a problem with the ground squirrel chewing wires to the television antenna on the roof, gnawing the plastic tubes coming from the swamp cooler, but now that the big Samoyed is around, the ground squirrel does not go on the roof.

It is a true pleasure seeing all of these Arizona animals getting along so well together.

The roadrunner who liked hamburger
By Helen Mallicoat
Wickenburg

This is a true story, but it didn't happen to me. It happened to a dear elderly couple who lived just across the street, Al and Vi. They noticed a roadrunner coming near their patio every afternoon around five. They decided to find out if he would eat hamburger.

They made little balls of it and put it out. Sure enough, the roadrunner loved it. They put some out every evening.

One time Al and Vi bought some cheap hamburger. The roadrunner wouldn't eat it.

Still, he came checking every evening. So they bought some more lean, and he ate it happily. They called him Henry.

Not long afterwards, they heard a pecking on their glass sliding door. There stood Henry with a dead lizard in his mouth. Al slowly opened the door. Henry walked in and laid his gift on the floor, then flew up on the table. Al got a picture of the bird. Henry spent a few more minutes going about the room, then walked out the open door.

Al and Vi have both gone to Heaven now, and I know they are happy for me to share this story with others who enjoyed their feathered and furry friends.

Close encounters of the furred kind
By Sylvia Dahlby
Cave Creek

I'm from Los Angeles, so I was ill-prepared for my first close encounters of the furred kind in Arizona. I had no idea the desert was so full of things. I'd lived in cities all my life. My idea of wildlife was pigeons, rats, and cockroaches.

On the day we moved into our new home we were greeted inside the front door by a large dead scorpion. Close inspection of the floors turned up three more scorpion corpses and one extra-large, super jumbo deluxe and alive tarantula. We immediately called an exterminator, but he couldn't come right now today.

We felt extremely nervous about sleeping on the floor that night. Our furniture would not arrive until the next day. We instructed our cats to stand guard as we bedded down on sleeping bags. I awoke in the middle of the night in the middle of a hounds-of-the-Baskervilles dream. Dozens—no, hundreds—of coyotes had the house surrounded. I woke my husband in a panic, crying, "What are they doing out there?"

My husband assured me that the coyotes weren't doing anything unusual and had not singled out our house for any kind of coyote attack. Nevertheless, I lay there and listened to them howl and yip for what seemed hours. I told myself that this was better than the sound of police sirens, and that I would get used to it. When the coyotes stopped, the quiet seemed even more eerie; this also would take some getting used to.

We began to settle in. I often sat on the back patio at sunset and watched the wildlife. I was enchanted by the quail, the cardinals, the wee beasties. I had no idea rabbits were wild animals—I'd thought them domestic like cats and dogs.

The wildlife took a lot of getting used to. The first time I saw a javelina, I was astonished at the size of it—and by the size of its teeth. With a cute little name like javelina, it created a vision of a much smaller piglet-like animal. I made it my business to learn more about the indigenous creatures so I wouldn't be as surprised or fearful.

One day I looked out the kitchen window to see a vulture in my concrete pond. I'd seen many wonders come for a drink, but this was my first vulture or turkey buzzard or whatchamacallit. It was beautiful in an ugly way. Soon it was joined by a second vulture. Then a third one perched in a tree to vultch over the other two. I figured there must be something dead or dying in the backyard. As I watched them, it felt they were watching me. This made me uneasy. It was creepy. I felt relieved when they finally took off.

It took a lot of getting used to. The snakes, the creepy crawlies, the furry beasties large and small. Now the surprises delight me: a glimpse of deer, jackrabbit, roadrunner, bird of prey. I'm not afraid of the wild creatures anymore. Now I know they fear me as one of the most dangerous creatures in the desert.

A mischievous raccoon
By Julie A. Jervis Brown, MD
Phoenix

My high school afternoons were spent as a veterinary surgical assistant in northern Arizona. One afternoon an hysterical woman brought in a challenge none of us would forget.

As the assistant, I was told to get an animal that had been hit on the highway from the woman's car. It was a large and beautiful male raccoon wrapped in bloody towels. He lay gasping for breath on the floor in back, his eyes begging for help. I picked him up gently and took him inside.

His main problem was a ruptured diaphragm, the muscle at the bottom of the ribs that makes you breathe. We went right into surgery. He became the first successful "traumatic diaphragmatic hernia repair" in a raccoon.

At first we were not sure he would survive. He simply lay in our intensive care unit bed wrapped in bandages. We gave him fluids and nutrition under his skin. After a week we removed his bandages. He became livelier by the day and before long a regular troublemaker.

He had incredible manual dexterity. He would soak a handful of his dried food in his water, then throw it at me. I worked with my back to him. He became so adept at his soggy food-throwing that he could stick a handful to my back without my knowing. Countless times I entered the examining rooms to pick up an animal from an owner for a treatment, only to be embarrassed by a glob of brown goo falling on the floor behind me.

The raccoon needed many X-rays to monitor his healing. He could not be held by the scruff of the neck, the way a raccoon is held, because of his surgery. My job was to get him to and from X-ray, holding his chest and abdomen. In this way, he had free rein to bite my hands. Every day that he needed an X-ray, I became a bloody pulp. He seemed to have forgotten the day he begged me for help.

The raccoon got well. He went home with our receptionist, who lived in the country. There, he proceeded to get hit by another car, opening his old injury. He returned for a second successful surgery, delighted to bite me and throw food at me again.

He recovered again and returned to Karla's house, where he took a wife and produced several generations of coons in the following years. He lived to a ripe old age and finally learned to stay away from cars.

The lions' lair
By Barbara Thompson
Cave Creek

In 1958 we met Shorty in Cave Creek. He came by one morning in hopes we would go along with him on a lion hunt to Buck Basin.

My children kept me tied to apron strings most of the time, while Rog in his free-roaming ways managed to be able and ready for adventure. *Adventure?* I wanted one. I needed one, and jumped at the chance, somehow knowing there'd be no lion in danger that day.

Shorty's old hound dogs, Mas and Blue, looked already tuckered in the late spring sun. Shorty was in his 80s. Raised by Indians near the Superstition Mountains, he had many a story to tell. Rog and his friend were happy to trip along, but not expecting to run into a lion.

We decided Shorty and I would stay behind while the younger men trailed with the hounds. We set set off for the winding dirt road to Buck Basin. Everything stood out vividly that day, strikingly bright and clear.

The approach to the basin's ridge opened like magic after a short hike from the truck. In we went to that wild place as to the garden of Eden.

The men seemed to disappear into the brush ahead. Left alone while Shorty rested, I followed a whim onto a large boulder for a better view of the deep, expansive canyon, lush and full of promise. With time now to drink in the beauty, I relaxed, breathing the scent of junipers.

As if on cue, a family of javelinas ambled by below. I soaked in the sight along with the sun. Soon a deer came by. Quail announced their presence. Maybe I was hallucinating in this pristine place. I let the spirit take me.

The next hour's wandering found me on the other side of the ridge near a huge mountain laurel tree on a knoll. Its full,

shining branches created a dome that reached to the ground. I hesitated in its presence, hoping to explore inside the cool shadows.

Suddenly, as if awakened from a dream, I heard a tremendous crashing of undergrowth. Who or what had charged away from this place I had invaded? I stood frozen, not wanting this wild world to end. I could not walk into that curtain of leaves. It now seemed a sanctuary forbidden to humans.

Descending the knoll with great reluctance, I followed a trail that turned back toward Shorty. As I approached him, he hollered out, "I saw that you flushed the biggest gray lion I've ever seen." I smiled an inward smile, feeling blessed and grateful.

The men and dogs soon showed up, weary from their trek, to hear how I had startled the lion they didn't shoot. The hunt was over and all was well. Each of us that day had a different story to tell.

Black widow
By Elizabeth Riordon
Hereford

The spider was actually quite beautiful. It was so black it shone like a piece of newly-broken obsidian in the sunlight. The scarlet marking on its underside was crisp and bright. The spider had made its home just behind the trash can, under the edge of the stucco.

We had lived here for about one year. Construction scared off the wildlife. The first welcome from the native animal life came from the little lizards. They sat in the afternoons decorating the wall. Too fast for the children to catch, the lizards let us get only close enough to wonder at their bead-patterned backs. When moth season arrived, the lizards feasted on the day-sleeping creatures hiding under the stucco edge. When they weren't looking for food, some of the lizards lived under the trash can, near the spider.

Once we caught a lizard. It had gotten trapped in a can on the porch. Excitedly, we put the little thing in our plastic bug box and kept it all evening on the dining room table. The night was too dark to go outside and let it go free, so we left that task for the morning. Sadly, the lizard did not survive the night. The bug box was made only for insects.

This morning the trash truck came early, before the rain. When we put the trash can back, one of the lizards did not move. Even when we reached out to touch it, it stayed still. Nearby lay three other tiny lizards, as still as their brother. Their heads had been opened, their brains eaten. Only one, who had been hiding behind a box, scurried off to safety. A few inches away from the miniature scene of carnage sat the fat black widow, shining in the sun.

Cat & rabbit friends
By Lisa L. Hall
Scottsdale

Nobody who is not prepared to spoil cats will get from them the reward they are able to give to those who do spoil them.
—Sir Compton Mackenzie, English writer

In November 1994 a benefit was held in Arizona on behalf of the Best Friends Animal Sanctuary, an animal shelter with more than 1,500 animal residents. The benefit was sponsored by The Classic Cat Gallery in Scottsdale. The principal activity of the benefit event was the first most-spoiled-cat-in-Arizona contest, a statewide competition open to all cats. The contest's celebrity judges—all fellow cat lovers—included Warren Iliff, director of the Phoenix zoo, Channel 3 television personality and author Jana Bommersbach, and author Eileen Bailey. The unanimous choice of the contest judges of the cat best suited to represent all of the spoiled felines in Arizona was Mango, a last-minute entry from the Pinnacle Peak area. Mango is a five-year-old female, tortoiseshell-point, Balinese-Himalayan cross.

The contest entry, limited to seventy-five words, simply read:

Of all the ways that we spoil Mango, the oldest and dominant cat of our current clowder of three cats, the most notable has been our allowing her to adopt her own housepet. Rhumba, a white lop rabbit, was abandoned as an adult by persons unknown about a year ago. We brought her home "temporarily," planning to find a home for her. Amazingly, Mango adopted the nine-pound orphan into our home. The two loving friends have been inseparable ever since.

It is sufficiently remarkable that these two Arizona creatures, Mango and Rhumba, represent two species that are natural enemies. Even more remarkable is the fact that they were fully mature adults when they met. These were not baby animals who had a chance to grow up together. This was not a case of imprinting. When Mango wraps her front paws around Rhumba's neck and scrubs away at Rhumba's dour little rabbit face with her sandpapery tongue, she is not grooming an animal she believes to be another cat or a kitten. She is grooming a rabbit.

When Mango purrs and talks to Rhumba, her vocalizations are not the same that she uses with our other two cats. When Mango allows Rhumba to lie with her head pressed tightly to Mango's body, she is accepting a gesture of rabbit affection, not a cat behavior. When Mango comes and gets me to come and feed her pet rabbit, she watches for me to get Rhumba's food (lettuce, parsley) out of the refrigerator, whereas she watches the kitchen cabinet when I get the cats' food.

In other words, Mango's affection for Rhumba cannot be explained away by the suggestion that she perhaps mistakes this rabbit for a cat. Rather, it is in simple fact just what it is: the affection of two friends for each other. They just happen to be rabbit and cat.

For the year ahead Mango will wear the title of most spoiled cat in Arizona, 1994-1995. She will wear it on behalf of thousands of homeless and unfortunate animals who will probably never be lucky enough to be spoiled. It is perhaps most appropriate that this particular cat will wear this title not really because of the care that she is given but because of the care and affection that she gives to others.

A frog speaks
By Oda L. Lomax
Chandler

I am just one voice, but I speak on behalf of millions. For as long as my species can remember, we have sacrificed our bodies in thousands of schools around the country in the name of science.

Millions of us have been taken from our natural habitats, crammed together in small boxes with no food, and have been transported great distances. This experience is extremely stressful for all of us because we are not accustomed to living in boxes.

When we reach our destination we are handled roughly and without any consideration for our well-being. We finally meet our fate through an injection of formaldehyde. Because most of us are fully conscious at this time, I must tell you that such an injection causes us much pain and distress.

So far, I have escaped this fate, and that is why I am able to tell my story. We serve a definite purpose on this Earth. When our populations dwindle—and, according to Jacques Cousteau, we are on a decline—insect populations rise, requiring an increased use of pesticides. It is well-known that pesticides are unhealthy for the environment and our wildlife, so why not leave the job to us?

Some years back, India exported millions of us each year, which created such havoc with that country's agricultural programs that it has since banned our export.

I am happy to say that many new and innovative techniques have been developed that should eliminate our slaughter. Computer programs, such as Visifrog, now are available to illustrate our internal structures. Plastic models, larger than life, beautifully reveal our anatomy. For younger students, there is Ribbit, a cloth frog that is quite adorable. Student-made models of human anatomy can be used as excellent teaching models as well. I could go on and on. The choices are endless and up to you.

We frogs, on the other hand, don't come cheap. A dozen of us costs from $70 to $120. Visifrog costs only $60 and can be used for many years.

After using us once, you will have to discard our bodies, an unpleasant task at best. When dead, I am not a pretty picture. When alive, I can teach you so much more about how and where I live, my reproduction, food chains, and interactions with the rest of the natural world.

I don't think it's too much to respect my right to live my life on this planet without harm or interference. I do not cause any harm, and I can benefit humanity much more when alive than dead. Dissecting me on a lab table is not a smart way to learn about me anyway.

If you haven't already guessed, this is a plea from me to you: Let me live. Respect my life as I respect yours. Is that too much to ask?

Oda Lomax is president of AWARE, Arizonans Working for Animal Rights through Education, 1730 West Linda Lane, Chandler, Arizona 85224; call 602.917.0041, fax -391.0888.

Father Peko
By Pat Lyon
Tucson

When Father Peko first presented himself to the chipmunk contingency on Windy Point, it was not exactly with his head held high. His rotund little figure in its patched habit tended to shuffle to and fro somewhat disconsolately as one in disgrace. In plain truth, he had been grounded for not adhering to the rules and regulations of the diocese above, namely the cathedral in the pines. Father Peko often had argued with himself that rules and regulations did not make a man's soul strong; only free will could do that. He knew himself to be weak, and

The blind squirrel & other Arizona animal tails

therefore presumptuous for having sworn to obey them in the first place. He was more ashamed of himself for that than for breaking rules.

Nothing else seemed to go on in the cathedral in the sky but beautiful psalmody sung by myriads of little fledgling choristers. For this, the frolicsome Windy Point contingency of chipmunks were expected to assemble below at specified times to hear the litany and receive the cardinal's blessing no matter what their cares and needs happened to be.

However, Father Peko soon began to prove his worth and be their real blessing. He turned out to be an excellent doctor with his potions and tinctures all gleaned from old Indian folklore, besides his duties of presiding at weddings and christenings and other events.

Father Peko's pipesmoking had been the main reason for his dismissal. He smoked dried mesquite leaves gathered from the desert below, then at odd moments.... Well, such a moment arose on his joyous return from delivering triplets: four bright-eyed furless babies. It suddenly came upon him to get out his pipe. He glanced up at the tall pine tops in order to assure himself he was not under surveillance, and, oh, he was, he was. There was the Red Cardinal taking a bird's eye view of the cheeky chipmunk community cavorting and frolicing below.

Tucking his pipe away, the little padre quickly dodged into the nearest rock crevice, namely Squeeze Belly Alley, and after a few ecstatic puffs of the beloved mesquite, which he breathed in deeply with his eyes closed, he made to move out again. But he was stuck. His protruding tummy could not budge. Just when he seemed to have been there for an eternity, little Gemima made her appearance in search of more turquoise powder for her paints.

"Oh, Father Peko, you startled me. Are you looking for turquoise, too?"

"Turquoise?" he gasped, and then, quickly, "Er, no, I was acquainting myself with the parish but had not reckoned on Squeeze Belly Alley being what it says it is."

In good earnest, Gemima suggested he breathe deeply to enable his chest to swell out and his tummy to draw in, but that didn't work. Next, she hit on the idea of pulling his robe as he breathed in. By now he was desperate and red in the face.

"Yes, yes, but please hurry. Evensong is about to begin, and if I'm not there with the people...." He breathed in, his tummy slightly receded, and in a flash Gemima pulled. Oh, glory be! His habit, already worn with age, ripped apart, revealing an uncouth pair of patched long johns. At least Father Peko was able to scrape himself out of his predicament, but only to find himself in a fresh one just as the cathedral bell tolled.

Holding the father's robe together, little Gemima hurried with him toward the waiting crowd. Looking up, they found the Red Cardinal still there on his balcony looking down in his usual unbenevolent manner. But now he summoned Father Peko to wait on him. There was their padre climbing the large cathedral pine like a miscreant sailor summoned before the mast. It was quite cruel and humiliating, and many a tear was shed from the normally frolicsome community below as his short, obese little figure puffed and panted up that huge pine, murmuring paternosters as he went.

Well, this little episode over but not forgotten, there came a beautiful moonlit evening when Mr. Chips and Antelope Jackrabbit toasted their toes before a log fire. They were just giving the Red Cardinal a good going over for about the sixth time, between sips of mulled ale, when Jack pricked up his ears and said, "Listen."

"What at?" said Mr. Chips. And then he heard. It was a far-away sequence of dull thuds.

"Someone's cutting down the trees again," said Jack, "but this time it's quite a ways from here."

The two of them deeming the act to be well out of danger to Windy Point, and leaving the fire to burn low, soon began to nod off in their chairs, when a sudden urgent knocking startled them awake.

Who should be at the door but Father Peko with a lantern, and holding a letter in his hand.

"Oh, Jack," he pleaded, "they are about to cut down the cathedral pine. There are men with saws out there now," and he began wringing his hands. But Antelope Jack was in no mood for solicitudes. He saw the act as the hand of Providence and began to laugh heartily as only wild jackrabbit rangers can.

They all raced down the long passage to the front door in time to hear the wild fluttering sounds of vacating cardinal and choristers above. Worse, the tree stealers already were applying the ax to the strong bark of the pine preparatory to using their huge electric saw.

"Well, well," said Jack, "proud stomachs are about to be brought low."

"Oh, please," pleaded Father Peko, handing Jack his letter. "You'll be in time if you run. Give this to Harry at the visitors' centre." Harry held a special place in his heart for the Windy Point contingency, and this they knew.

Reluctantly, Antelope Jack, fastening up his leather-fringed jacket, tucked the letter in his dispatch satchel.

"Okay, get out of my way, both of you." Taking a few athletic leaps across the mountainside, he was up and on the road like lightning.

Time and space forbid detailing all that happened, except to say that all that we hoped would happen really did. The culprits were apprehended in best forest ranger fashion just as the electric saw was placed in position. They were hauled off to you know where, after which peace and harmony was restored to Windy Point.

Postscript

Try to imagine Father Peko and Antelope Jack climbing the cathedral pine together midst a volley of cheers and hurrahs from below. Imagine also the two heroes hugged and kissed on both cheeks by a tearful yet joyful Red Cardinal, then taken to be wined and dined and commended. Then imagine the pair appearing together on the balcony later with Father Peko newly robed, the songs and chants this time coming up from the frolicsome community below instead of from above down, and the sun from out of a blue sky pronouncing its benediction on them all.

The conspiracy of silence
By Pat Lyon

It was a beautiful autumnal day on the mountain, not too hot nor too cold. The little chipmunks were seated in rows with their slates watching Mr. Chips in his cap and gown drawing maps on the blackboard. Every now and then they heard visitors' cars draw up to the overlook and families get out to admire the view. In their eagerness to be out there on the rocks sporting themselves for the sake of cookies and popcorn, the little furry scholars could hardly keep still in their seats.

The lesson was about a famous mountain abounding in tales, and legends of fairies and animals, where an Indian tribe had lived peaceably for many years until, until....

"However," said Mr. Chips, turning to face the class and putting his chalk down, "great sorrow eventually came to the people on the mountain. And why? Can anyone guess why?"

No paw went up in the air. He glanced hopefully at the sprightly little faces but their ears were cocked in the direction of the visitors. A little chipmunk called Jasimine whispered concernedly to a friend, "I hope Rocky and his gang don't get to the popcorn before us. I get so bored with plain nuts." Rocky and Company were rock squirrels, larger and tougher, with no softness in their fur at all. No visitors ever said of them, "Aren't they cute?" but the squirrels took more than their share of all the goodies.

Mr. Chips now perceiving Jasimine's consternation appealed to her. "Jasimine, what could happen to a people on a mountain that could bring much sorrow and change their lives completely?"

In her overexuberance she blurted out, "Oh, please, sir, they could close the road to all visitors and then, and then there'd be no more...no more—" She faltered and Mr. Chips helped her.

"—No more cookies and popcorn, you were about to say?"

At this, all the little scholars laughed. He turned to the class. "Oh dear, oh dear, then you would all sleep all week long and every week, instead of coming awake on Fridays. There would be nothing to wake up for, would there?"

At this, little Billyboy, the goody-two-shoes of the class, spoke up. "We would, sir, we'd want to hear more stories about other countries instead of men coming with pick axes and drills looking for copper and gold. Mr. Chips, sir, would they come and tear up our mountain like that just for turquoise?"

"Turquoise, Billy?" Mr. Chips was mystified "Well, er, yes, they could. Turquoise stone is very precious for making jewelry. Indians wore such finery a great deal, and now silversmiths are paying quite a—" He was interrupted by all eyes staring at the back of the class in Gemima's direction. She, bedecked as usual in her frills and ribbons, was scratching away at her slate with something chalky the exact colour of turquoise. The sudden silence in the room caused her to look up startled, and then Mr. Chips realized what she was holding.

"Good gracious, Gemima" he gasped, his pince-nez spectacles nearly falling off the end of his nose. "Where did you get that from?" He picked the turquoise up and examined it minutely. "Squeeze Belly Alley," she told him innocently.

"Does anyone else besides those of us here know of this?"

"Oh, no," said Gemima. "See! If you mix it with water it makes nice water colour for pretty pictures," and she showed him a little painting.

Looking up and noticing the consternation on the various faces, Mr. Chips said kindly, "This kind of turquoise is only worth the pleasure it can afford you children in drawing and painting. It is too soft for the making of jewelry, and therefore you need not fear the possibility of any mining here." This was met with sighs of relief and much joviality.

"I began by asking you children a question which none of you seemed inclined to answer. However, my telling you that turquoise stone was considered valuable enough to merit opening up the sides of a mountain really set you all thinking and worrying, didn't I?"

By now the little scholars had ceased to notice the visitors' cars drawing up on the overlook. Nor did they care about the funny food. All that concerned them was the fact that their dear mountain was safe and that people would in the future heed the notices which the forest rangers, who protected all the animals, had installed everywhere, saying briefly and to the point, *This is Nature—Respect it!*

Other animals, other stories

A tremendous tarantula

Coming home at 10:30 after an evening at the Heard Museum in Phoenix, where I looked up some old relatives, I approached my front door and stopped. Near the concrete slab and in a corner formed by the entry hall and a north-facing bedroom, a tarantula clung to the wall. Possibly he had been attracted by small moths attracted by twin porch lights. This was a real tarantula, the kind you see in zoos or in clear plastic cubes, at least three inches long with arms drawn in, a heavy, hairy beast unlike the lightweights I'd squashed in the bathroom. When I encounter an errant spider in the house, I usually grab a paper-bound book on minerals. It is heavy enough to flatten any spider. (A book about feathers would not work.) This tarantula looked so big, though, that had I swatted at him with the book he would have grabbed it out of my hands, torn out all the pages, and thrown them back at me. Squatting down, I approached within three feet of the spider and gently blew on him. He cringed but did not move. My mouthwash, I decided, was holding. Quietly, gently, I unlocked the door, said goodnight, and double-locked it behind me.

That cat was a dog

We saw giant footprints in the driveway of what must have been a mountain lion. Daughter Lizz came for a visit in early April, saw our plaster casting of one of the prints, and laughed. Much closer to animals than I, she said, "This is a dog. Look at the big toenails."

She is the expert. I would not want to meet the 300- to 400-pound dog who belongs to the footprint, however. On a hunch, I called *Parade* magazine.

"By chance," I asked, "is your Howard Huge missing?"

"Why, yes, he is," said the cartoon editor. "How did you know? We've been trying to keep it quiet."

I gave him my address. Perhaps we'll see people with cages and nets in the valley soon. In the meantime I'm re-reading Tom Brown's book, *The Tracker,* paying particular attention to the illustrations.

Birth control for wasps

For the past three weeks a pair of wasps has been trying to build a nest in which to lay eggs. They selected a shaded site under the roof of my balcony, with a good view of the mountains to the north. Wanting to discourage the wasps, I took yardstick in hand and, just after dusk, played fencer. The inch-long paperlike nest fell to the deck, the wasps still attached to it. Their vision in dim light was not sufficient for them to see their attacker. I thought my ploy would send them seeking a new site the next morning. I was wrong. Three more times they attempted to rebuild, and three more times I lunged at their nest, each time giving them a few more days to work before the destruction. One evening I heard a buzzing on the deck and went to investigate. Apparently unable to wait for a nest to receive the female's fertilized eggs, the two wasps writhed in pleasure on the deck, legs locked, wings buzzing, ends of abdomens probing. A voyeur, I merely watched. How do wasps make love? V-e-r-y carefully.

A farewell to legs

Lately we've suffered from an ant problem. The tiny beasts, barely a millimeter in length, have been marching into the kitchen. At first they swarmed over a plastic bottle of honey, licking their chops or whatever it is they lick. They died suddenly when I sprayed them with the blue window cleaner everyone keeps. Apparently the alcohol knocked them right out and they did not come back. I sprayed their single-file rank where it ran across a corner of the kitchen floor and under the door.

    Ants own a certain small intelligence. Though sightless, they communicate with each other in little dances. I figured the survivors would get the message about the massacre and take off. They didn't. The next day they were back, looking for the honey that now sat in its bottle inside a sealed plastic bag. I looked at one under a magnifying lens. It wore a T shirt on which was scrawled, "I SURVIVED THE BLUE SPRAY!"

    Outside, the line of little ants went under the back porch and down the steps—not the way you and I do it but on the sides and undersides of the steps. I traced their line across the remains of a stone wall and into the front yard. They'd marched at least fifty feet from their nest by the driveway. For a millimeter-long ant, that distance represents roughly twenty of our miles. They moved fast, never stopping for beer. They couldn't stop to appreciate the view across the sideyard to the fence. They walked the equivalent of you or me walking from Cave Creek to New River. Most of it in the shade, but still! Who knows how many trips each ant made per day? They didn't move at night, for some reason. Bigger red ants with at least vestigial eyes took over at night.

Well, I solved the ant problem by moving the honey to them. Each day I've been pouring a little right by their nest. They don't need to walk as far now. They stay out of the kitchen. Of course, there's a downside to this generosity, and it's not in the ants' favor. They've grown lazy. In just a few generations their legs aren't as strong, I notice. A lot of them don't bother to come out of the nest anymore, preferring to sit back and watch the ant olympics on television, I suppose. It happened to humans. Medical researchers now say that metropolitan man (and woman) has lost 0.003 per cent of muscle tissue from left legs and feet since the advent of the automatic transmission in the 1950s.

And the big trouble is yet to come: An ant-eating woodpecker, a flicker, has been eyeing the ants and their nest. It's only a matter of time. See how man intrudes on nature even with the best of intentions?

If you know the theme from "Moonlighting," sing along:
None walk by night, some walk by day;
Something is sweeter that we left in their way...

Javelina mine

Maybe you know that soft song, "Ballerina, Girl"? Its first four syllables can be replaced by *javelina,* pronounced in the desert as if it started with an *h* instead of a *j*. The javelina is a peccary that strayed far north. It roots around the desert at night. A strict vegetarian, the javelina can run its tough snout into the packed sand of a wash in search of succulent roots. I tell you these things so that you can better judge for yourself if the following story might own some truth. A long-time resident of Cave Creek told us the story. He has high credibility but he also leaves fake messages on phone answering devices, so one never knows.

These two machos went hunting for javelina. (There is a brief season when they're legally killed.) They shot two animals, gutted them, and cut off the heads. When they happened to look in the mouths, the glint of

gold flashed back at them. Some sick animal dentist had filled the teeth of the lower jaws with gold. Or so it appeared. After thinking about it for a while, the brave hunters realized that the javelinas probably got the gold from rooting in the sand of dry river beds. The sand slobbered out or was swallowed; the gold, because it is malleable, squashed down between the teeth. My source says that the layer of gold lay so thin that a rainstorm washed the gold away when one of the hunters left his booty outside to age. Knowing how often it rains here in the desert, I'm suspicious.

Some strange names for mines appear on maps around here. One is called Mormon Girl, another Go John. Now, at least in the mind of a storyteller, another portable gold mine lurks in the nighttime shadows: Javelina mine.

The blind squirrel & other Arizona animal tails

Javelina, mine,
   Your teeth are sparkling:
Eighteen carats fine;
   Come here, you darkling.

Diatomaceous dialog

The Jurassic period ended a long time ago. Where we live in Arizona is a floor of ancient seas, which explains why I sometimes feel nauseous. The only life in the seas of that early time were one-celled organisms, early algae and a tough-shelled little bugger called the diatom. We use diatoms today to filter things and to make the subtle grit in our toothpaste. They haven't been alive for millions of years, but they still go to work for us.

Like viable, refriable Anasazi beans found in a dry cave in a ceramic jar where a little old woman stored them 800 years ago, some of the diatoms managed to survive the drying up of their sea. They became reconstituted when supplied with water in a septic tank outside the home of Jason and Peggy Williamson in Cave Creek, on the north slope of Black Mountain. With sophisticated electronic snooping gear, I was able to record some of the diatoms' conversations. They apparently had learned intraspecies communication during their long, dry sleep. Here, with some editing, are a few of their more sensible responses to their environment.

Tom the Diatom: "I'm sure glad Jason gave up oil painting. All that turpentine down the tubes gave me the willies. What a stench. I'm so glad he's sticking with water colors."

Diane the Diatom: "You're so fussy. Say, would you rub my back with your flagella— My back, Tom! My back! Oh, you." (Later, Diane admitted she could tell by taste the predominant color coming out of Jason's brush when he washed it.)

Some simple bacteria came into the conversation, too, apparently having learned how to communicate with their superiors, the diatoms, who feast on bacteria. Through my instruments, I could hear them hum and cough just like you and me.

Jerry the Germ: "I hear the town is going to run sewers just about everywhere. Where do think that will leave us?"

Herm the Germ: "Where do you think? We'll have to hang on to the diatoms and swim upstream with them."

Jerry: "Yeah? Where do think upstream is?"

Herm: "In the house?"

Jerry: "Damn right. Not too far to go. Not too much to eat there, either. Me, I'd flow with the stream. I wouldn't mind taking a trip down the hill."

Herm: "To where? You'd get burned out in a disposal plant. You don't take well to sun tans. Har, har."

One thing I learned about microscopic conversations: They exist on a level with those in many coffeeshops.

A clash of worlds

We species keep to ourselves, generally. We don't even talk one species to another. Nor for all our vaunted super intelligence, we humans don't even understand what the other species are saying. We often call their sounds noise, a distraction, sound without meaning. To us.

Even robins don't talk to sparrows. And certainly thrushes don't speak to cowbirds. An eagle might squawk at a vulture, but he won't tell him where to find the freshest dead cow. Humans speak to their dogs and cats, but there's no hard evidence that the pets understand much beyond a few simple commands. And, smart as we are, we don't understand half a syllable our dogs and cats spout at us. (Although, that said, I must say I communicated with a dumb dog in Colorado last summer while helping build a mountainside cabin with our daughter Lizz. In the back of my truck were a pile of 2x6 firestops, cut to go between wall studs. The hike, though only fifty feet up the mountain at 7,500 feet above sea level, was exhausting. Lizz's two dogs ran up and down it with ease. We who live at 2,300 feet panted and turned blue. As a joke I grabbed one of the stops, shoved it in the mouth of the dumb dog, and urged him up the hill. To my surprise, he ran all the way up to the cabin, dropped the wood, and came back. He made ten such trips, and I photographed him doing it, because no one would believe it without evidence. We called him the dumb dog because the other dog was smart. The smart one refused to touch the wood. Why should he work?)

Man talks to computers, but then such machines are an extension of man. While it's possible to speak words to certain computers now, most of the talking is done with the fingers, on a keyboard, making words.

What brings up the subject of transspecies communication is a need for it lately. This week ten-year-old friend Amelia spotted a javelina by the corral. We hurried down to see it. There stood the collared peccary (its name in English) with its face buried in weeds. I walked up to it, took a few pictures, approaching within three feet. The others in the viewing party shrank back and warned me. The javelina did not wish to communicate with me, though, and went on hiding. It was as if, because he could not see me, then I did not exist. The ostrich syndrome. That isn't like javelinas. Usually nocturnal, they're smart enough to avoid we ugly bipeds. They're also highly social, traveling in herds. This one stood alone.

Vicente, who used to live where I do now, had stopped by to check the horses and noticed the javelina. He thought something was wrong with it and used my phone to call the state's game and fish department. They were interested. They'd send out a man. Vicente waited all afternoon, tracking the javelina's movements up and down the wash.

The man arrived in a pickup truck toting a huge steel cage. His business card read, *Russell A. Haughey, Wildlife Manager.* Vicente led him to the javelina, now lolling on his back between two rocks, panting, not bothering to flick away gnats around his eyes. The man eased a loop of steel wire around the javelina's neck, then pulled with a metal pole. The apparently dying animal sprang to life, dug in his hooves, excreted musk from the gland on his back, squealed, but ended up in the cage.

"We don't know what it is," Russell explained. "We'll get him to the U of Arizona in

Tucson and maybe they'll find out. They want a specimen before he dies. It might be a kind of canine distemper." The pickup roared away down the wash and off to a road.

Others in the past week reported strange behavior from ordinarily wild and wily javelinas. A week earlier Tom Blaney approached a javelina walking around and around a pond of water on Military Road. Water around here is rare enough to cause curiosity, but the animal did not flee when Tom approached. Tom was able to touch it. We hope Tom does not have distemper.

Steve McNeil tells of a hike to the top of Black Mountain with Irma Turtle just last week. Irma sat down to rest. A female javelina walked up and put its head in her lap. Two days later Steve climbed back up. He found the javelina on the trail, dead.

My Jane, driving on Piedra Grande, which connects Cave Creek with Carefree, jammed on the truck's brakes when a javelina sauntered out on the road in broad daylight, taking no notice of the big cream-colored Ford. Jane thought that behavior strange.

I wish the sick animals could have told us more, but that's the trouble. They can't. That is why veterinarians have a harder job than human doctors: patients can't describe their own symptoms.

The day after the javelina was carted off to Tucson we enjoyed a visit from a rattlesnake.

Nancy, who'd been using a copier in my office, came down to the house to tell of the snake. She came quickly out a side door that had not been opened in three years. The snake lay coiled in a doorway where the door stood open to let in the fresh air of springtime. I ran up to look, and, no, she was not joking, and, yes, it was a rattlesnake. He (snakes are always *he* unless proven otherwise) was about three feet long, though you don't want to measure them accurately. He bore the telltale arrow-shaped head and came with full rattling equipment. Snakes reproduce in the springtime; he'd obviously seen my Minolta copier through the open door.

I grabbed a plastic gas pipe and tried to nudge the snake toward me and out the door. He wasn't having any. He slithered under a closet door and behind three old twelve-volt boat batteries. Gingerly, I pulled one of the batteries out. No snake. No room behind the other batteries for a snake. He must have gone elsewhere.

I'd always wanted to work in the cool house instead of the office, to see what it was like. Maybe, if I left the door open, the snake would return to its world. Maybe three more snakes would come in and start a poker game.

The next morning there was no sign of a snake, but then snakes don't make big signs to say hello or goodbye. I returned to work on my computer in the office, turning my head now and then for any sign of movement in my peripheral vision. I half expected to feel something cold and muscular wrap itself around my leg just to get warm. Nothing. But as I left the office, the familiar head stuck out from under the closet door and a dull, irritated rattling began.

Nancy suggested putting some kind of powder down, where the snake could leave a trail, as a means of letting us know whether he'd left yet. I found a bag of weevil-infested flour and sprinkled it in a semi-circle around the closet door and on the threshold nearby. After lunch I came back up to the open door. The flour had been written upon by the snake, clearly and cleanly. His path through the flour came from closet and across threshold. Or was it the snake's mate coming in to join the game?

To discourage such events in the future I've put a sign near the bottom of my office door:

VERTEBRATES
WITHOUT FEET
NOT WELCOME

I know there's this problem of cross-species communication, but I keep hoping. Before he left, the snake somehow pecked out a note on my computer keyboard:

"the rat was good but the flour was awful. —lyle"

I don't expect we'll see him again. Species can, of course, communicate among their own kind, and I hope Lyle will.

Viewer discretion advised

At the end of a social evening of dinner outside and light talk, we entered the kitchen to find two disturbed pre-teens, Amelia and her friend Kim.

"Oh," groaned Amelia, "I didn't want to see that."

It was too late to turn off the television, far too late to ask why she had not switched channels or left the room. She had seen a segment of "20/20" dealing with the uncaring people who breed pets in quantity in horrible conditions for resale. As usual, a governmental agency, the US department of agriculture, the same ones who mismanage our national forests, played one of the culprits.

As we left the house, Amelia said to her mother, "I think I'm going to throw up." All of us expressed concern, but, once out the door, I said I was glad she was physically moved by what she'd seen—and that she'd seen tortured and sick animals. From that moment on pets would have new meaning. From then on the gap between what people say and what they do would catch her daydreaming, would keep her awake, attentive, to her dog and her gerbils and whatever other pets would come into her life.

I knew all that not because I'm old and smart but because I have a daughter to whom that happened. It may not have been an exposé on television, but likely one excruciating event made Lizz respond violently. Since then she has never been the same—and animals' lives have been the better for her discomfort because she has become a leading animal rights' activist.

I think the others were horrified at the Friday night's television entertainment, but I was pleased. One day Amelia may find pleasure in such sudden, ugly learning. It is, after all, how we grow up in America, and Amelia is pushing eleven.

A desert foothills natural calendar

(Eat it when you've finished reading.)
With contributions from Geoffrey Platts and Eleanor Radke

January
Constellation Orion stands overhead at dusk

February
Jojoba in flower, such as they are
First signs of deervetch, windflowers, cliffrose

March
Ocotillo in flaming scarlet flower
Mesquite leafs out, flowers
Vultures (*zopilotes*, the Mexican highway patrol) return
Snow has been seen in some years

April
Palo verde trees burst into delicate yellow flowers

May
Saguaros show white blossoms
Phainopeplas (a black flycatcher) head north for the summer, some only 1,000 feet, none too soon
Ironwoods put out lavender blossoms

June, July, August
Saguaros show magenta fruit
Night-blooming cereus blossom sneaks out one night only
Monsoons may attack, starting in July
Rocks melt
Long-inactive volcanoes have second thoughts

September
Snowbirds begin southern migration
Blankets may be needed again
Poorwills think of hibernation, our only bird to sleep away the winter

October
Vultures leave for better pickin's
White-crowned sparrows return
Earth Rallies herself in Cave Creek (an annual eco fair)
Ether appears in gasoline for the winter in Maricopa county

November
Rattlers usually sleep until March (not guaranteed)

December
Mesquite leaves fall as yellow-brown confetti
Creosote bush, Earth's oldest living being, erupts with yellow blossoms, followed by white fuzzballs of seeds
Phainopeplas return in profusion, to perch on mistletoe so that you can kiss them at Christmas

Ecodisaster strikes our ecofair

Earth Rally II, Geoffrey Platts called it, a reprise of the event of last year when the environmentally slick community of Cave Creek sought to upgrade the Neanderthals in Scottsdale and Phoenix. The indefatigable Platts ran his engine all day, coaxing an unlikely admixture of Sierra Club and US forest service, hawking a Nature walk, and talking up a competing event in the community, OctoberWest, which is not misspelled. That Saturday night Platts found new energy somewhere and read to a flock of the fascinated. He ought to be in Hollywood; his enemies say he ought to be back in England. Nonetheless, Earth Rally II triumphed over a grudging, insolent view that everything is all right in Nature if we just keep on polluting. You could look around the tamarisk grove and see hair standing on end from all the consciousness-raising. Short people had to worry about banging into the branches of the water-hungry trees that some think ought to be murdered. Others think the trees wonderful for the thin shade they produce.

    Our son Mark put together a booth of found objects to help upgrade viewers about local water problems. Mark used Tom Blaney's blownup photos (which Mark had found under a rock) of Desert Mountain Development, a burgeoning community five miles northeast of Cave Creek that legally sprays no less than one million gallons of aquifer-drawn water daily on its three golf courses. Mark sought to inform those who passed by his booth.

It worked well, right up until the end. Geoffrey had written a proclamation directed at two of our state legislators, asking them to consider revising the law that allows developers such as Desert Mountain to take as much water as they want from limited resources. Perhaps 2,000 persons passed by over the weekend, reading photo captions, asking questions, expressing amazement at what evil developers can do when developing Sonoran desert into Disney desert, as Geoffrey likes to call it. We heard no one defend golf. Many expressed disgust at its effects.

Then trouble hit. A gust of wind toppled Mark's plywood exhibit onto the Adobe Mountain Wildlife Rehabilitation Center display just to the east. The plywood broke a glass cage containing about ten packrats. Almost blinded by the sunlight, the little nocturnal vermin nonetheless scrambled toward anything dark. Women screamed. A great-horned owl, nursing a broken wing, found strength in its good arm and half-flew, half-ran at the fleeing rats. In a nearby booth a man wearing a docile python around his neck and shoulders found the snake a sudden slither of activity. The eighteen-foot-long beast spilled across the ground like water flowing downhill, heading for the rats. Glomp, glomp, glomp. It was over in seconds. No pack rat remained, but ten lumps traveled slowly away from the python's head. Then, spotting the big owl, the python coiled and shot out for dessert. A flurry of round-edged feathers was all that remained when the snake hiccoughed. The quick attack had not missed the eyes of the Floresta. The forest service men and two women ran from their booth and confronted the now-dozing python. One pulled his gun and held it at the snake's head. The snake's handler ran up and threw himself on the ground beside the python.

"Don't you hurt my little Saucisson!"

The red-faced Floresta man put away his gun and returned to his booth.

After that, nothing much exciting happened.

Cloning the dinosaur

The news must have shaken the scientific world: A researcher posits that he can find something within an insect preserved in amber, an insect which feasted upon a dinosaur in long-ago times. What he would find would be a cell, perhaps a blood cell, of the dinosaur. From deep within the cell, the scientist would scrape away a fleck of DNA. Building on this building block, the scientist figures he should be able to bring to life a whole dinosaur. He can't stop there, of course; if his creation is a male, he will have to keep making more until he finds a female, for the male will want to reproduce.

(Imagine your embarrassment when a loose male humps your antique Volkswagen Beetle. The body repair guy laughs and says, "Ho, ho. Diddled by a dino, eh? You should keep this in a garage.")

You get the picture. Soon we can forget unhealthy, fatty beef and dig into some genuine reptile. Because some scientists forecast a demise of all life in the seas by 2000 due to pollution, it will be good to have an alternative food source available.

I'd like to own a herd of *Tyrannosaurus rexes*. So would any kid who has seen their pictures. Because these beasts are bigger than anything else that has ever walked the earth, they'll require extra heavy fencing—and a big food source. We could start with the walled golf courses of Arizona, and maybe train the dinos to like grass even though some think they all were carnivores. When the place had been eaten back to original desert, the beasts would have to go elsewhere.

Why not to our national forests, where today privately-owned cattle destroy whatever lives there and create massive erosion with their indelicate hooves? The rangers at the Cave Creek district of Tonto National Forest better prepare an application that grants permission to me to run my herd on public lands. The dinos wouldn't range too far, of course. They might like saguaros, so you could expect them to stay below 3,500 feet and to never stray as far south as Sun City should they break out of the forest's boundary fence. We've all seen cattle guards. Can you imagine a dinosaur guard? Maybe a ferry could float your car across.

The dinosaurs, in any concentration, would cause a problem on a scale equivalent to that of their bovine brethren: dinosaur doo-doo. Just keep in mind when knocking dinos that the pile of rock we today call The Boulders is nothing more than a pile of fossilized dinosaur excrement. Perhaps we can train the beasts to carry a roll of t.p. to the county land fill to do their dirty business.

Who knows? It might work. I'm willing to give up vegetarianism for a dinosaur steak.

A letter to public television

Sirs:

I have come to expect more of you than what I see on commercial television. You disappointed me tonight with your pre-halloween special on serpents. We saw the mating dance of a pair of adders, and then a closeup of them doing It while the announcer told us that all male snakes have two of Them and can stay inserted for up to three hours. (That makes six hours per snake.) What unadulterated prurience.

With no warning you show a picture like that while my twenty-nine-year-old son stands next to me with eyes bugging out as we fight for a closer view of the screen. Never mind that you followed it with lots of scenes of egg-laying. You might have warned us at the beginning so that we could have turned away or switched channels. Suddenly It was there. The British Broadmindedcasting Company might have substituted a shot of a bee rubbing a flower. How do I explain to my son what we saw—and closeup, and in color?

What can we expect next from you? Horses or dogs doing It? Is that part of your program to bring live human mating to the tube? To beat commercial television at naughtiness?

And just as I was whipping out my checkbook to make good on my million-dollar pledge (contingent upon my winning of the lottery) you commit such a visual sin before my eyes. Let's make it a rule: no undressed snakes on television. They're just too suggestive. We don't need further overstimulation of our youth. For shame, Channel Eight.

Animal wrongs

The rage today is for people to espouse animal rights. My daughter Lizz devotes much of her life to the rights of dogs, cats, harp seals, and any needy fur- or feather-bearer. While I generally agree with Lizz, I think our society may have gone too far. Just today I saw a bumper sticker that read
    NUKE GAY WHALES FOR JESUS
It was sort of your generic, composite bumper sticker, but I could read into it the disgust of a whole generation of Americans who've had it up to their mink hats with animal rights. It's time we looked at some animal wrongs.

Take the case of Mrs. Gladys Goldfinch of Epitak, Kansas. Barely able to walk after hip surgery at age seventy-five, Mrs. Goldfinch doddered along her garden walk last June. Her failing eyesight did not let her see a convention of snails, probably gathered to discuss what to do about Central America and killer bees. She slipped on the slimy mass of snails, fell, broke her other hip, and has been in traction for almost a year. Some bleeding hearts will feel sorry for those snails, who admittedly lost a lot of cousins and grandparents, but not me. I say the snails should be seen as trespassers. The snails had not been invited on Mrs. Goldfinch's property. They paid no taxes. They contributed to her well-being in no conceivable way. Yet there they slimed when she took a well-intentioned walk, minding her own business. Maybe they should have died. I know that statement will shock the animal rights activists, but that's the mood of the country right now.

Recently I was involved in a divorce trial heard before a blind judge. At his feet throughout the two-week trial sat a huge dog, intimidating to everyone but animal rights activists and the judge. My lawyer's daughter, like Lizz one of those dog lovers from birth, tried to send bones to the dog by wrapping them in plastic and hiding them in her father's briefcase, but he caught on before he could be cited for contempt or attempted bribery. The trouble with this dog was that he thought he was so damn smart. Whenever a witness lied, the dog seemed to know it. He would stand up and wail until the judge smacked him on the head with a gavel. The dog's performance disturbed the courtroom scene no end and put the fear of torn clothing into witnesses. Had any of the lawyers suggested the dog influenced the trial, the judge might have said nothing, but that lawyer could forget about practicing in that county anymore.

Animal rights are all right in their place, but there are a lot of places—gardens and courtrooms among them—where animals shouldn't have any rights at all. As a former editor of mine was saying the other night as he bit into a slab of shark at a seafood restaurant, "It's only fair. They eat us, so I eat them." I seconded that sentiment. "Fish don't have any rights, anyway," I said, knowing my daughter would not approve. Watch out, America. Next thing, they'll want to drive cars and vote.

Messages from Mother Nature

The lizards around our home seem to come in just two kinds, short and long. I've been puzzling about that phenomenon for some time. Yesterday, while lunching at the Blue Bird on a tuna sandwich, I wrote out a check for twenty-five dollars to Greenpeace, the organization that saves whales, dolphins, and other life, and seems more activist than the Sierra Club. As I sealed the envelope with the check inside, an insight flashed: The lizards might be trying to send me a message.

So I started to keep track of the order in which I saw the lizards as they darted across my front yard. I used a simple code, S for short and L for long. When a dozen lizards had done their dance, I tried to break up the shorts and longs into intelligent Morse code. It came down to this:

UPYORZ

I'm still tallying and will keep you advised.

A visit from the "children"

From the offspring? From the descendants? *Children* does not describe the twenty-three-year-old daughter and twenty-seven-year-old son who visited in May for their grandfather's eightieth birthday reunion. Lizz came first, driving down non-stop from the mountains of northeast Colorado to the foothills of central Arizona, two dogs roaming aimlessly in her little red Honda. She could tolerate only two days away from her menagerie on the shores of the Poudre River northwest of Fort Collins, where she works for the local humane society parttime and dabbles at veterinary medicine fulltime at Colorado State University. Lizz streaked out of Cave Creek on a Thursday evening, her cheeks flushed, her heart beating fast with the rush of Coca-Cola caffeine. Only one dog went back with her.

Mark arrived at Sky Harbor airport in Phoenix at about the same hour he really awakens at home in Roseville, Michigan, midnight. Jane and I met the Northwest flight, then rushed him to Sun City, where some of Mark's ancestors sat up talking about old times in the caves of southern Illinois at the turn of the millenium. Mark missed a chance to talk to his sister by about twenty-four hours. Too bad. But that way there was no need to share grandparents.

The morning after Lizz's arrival, Jane and I took her in the pick-up truck to a place we call Petroglyph Canyon, a narrow, water-cut gorge, a sacred spot flanked by vertical basalt cliffs on which Native Americans created startling graffiti. On the way down the horse trail to the canyon, with Lizz and her dog leading the way, we heard her shout.

"Dad! There's a rattler! Omgnu! Come here!"

Omgnu is the dog's name. The *g* is silent, but the dog is not. The dog sniffed out the snake, but retreated when Lizz called it. (The dog used to be a female.)

We stopped. A sound like that made by a punctured water line came from just off the trail. Lizz pointed. We looked. The snake, coiled back on itself, its heat sensor flicking, sat on a bare spot of hillside where likely it had been warming itself in the morning sun. It was as thick as a heavy mooring line, and the color of red granite, with irregular dark brown spots.

"Shall I throw a rock?" Lizz asked.

"No," I said. "This is his home. Let's just leave the trail for a few feet and then come back to it." The hissing noise of dry rattles shaking continued. It was the first live rattler I'd seen in more than two years of hiking around these foothills. We walked carefully after that, more slowly, more discerningly checking out roots and branches that curved.

When we arrived at what I call the entrance, a narrowing in the canyon where the first petroglyphs soar like a school kid's blackboard drawing, I looked up to point them out with my hiking stick. Far above the canyon, an owl glided, disappearing behind a rock. We continued, with Jane and I as tour guides, Lizz as interested observer with plenty of background in the bio sciences.

On another foray, we drove Lizz and one of the dogs, Tigger, a two-and-one-half-year-old "mixed" breed, to Sun City, where Lizz presented the overgrown lap dog to her grandfather as a birthday gift. The grandparents, who had not owned a dog in about ten years and who were ready for one again, according to Lizz, said nothing but shut the doors from the kitchen to the rest of the house. Lizz was thorough. She provided an automatic waterer and dog dish and a return warranty: If they didn't want the dog after trying it (formerly a female) for a month, they could drop it off at Lizz's place on their way north to Idaho for the summer. Lizz knew what would happen.

 When Mark arrived, we whisked him to the canyon, too, so he could sense its magic. He drove the Ford truck over one of the oldest roads in Arizona, according to Nancy Zeno, and in places where you aren't sure any road exists. He broke no springs and punctured no tires. Neither did he flush a rattler. We took care to creep down the trail.

 When we entered the sacred region, I pointed again with my stick—and there flew the owl again. It surely was a sign. Perhaps it meant something physical: The owl wanted to undergo an operation from Lizz so it would never again have to lay those ugly, little miniature ping-pong balls. Or maybe something magic lay in its soaring as we entered its home territory.

After both descendants had gone back to their workaday worlds, Jane and I received as visitors a couple, distant relatives of hers from Ann Arbor, Michigan. We led them into the canyon, too. No snakes, no owl. But farther up the canyon than we'd walked with either Mark or Lizz I found a feather from the owl, as if she couldn't be bothered this time, but here was a token. Maybe Lizz is right. Her guiding philosophy for years has been that you can't trust people but you can trust animals. She spends most of her efforts on those who do not speak with words.

Back in Sun City, shortly after Mark left, the doors to the kitchen stayed open. Tigger moved throughout the house and at last look was now sleeping in bed with Grandma and Grandpa. Lizz knew it.

Headline: "Idaho hunters enjoy record season"

"The harvest is the highest on record, and reflects the health of our elk population," Idaho Fish and Game big game manager Lonn Kuck said. "For elk hunters, these are the good old days."

And for the elk?

That verb, *harvest,* intrigues me. So euphemistic, so unreal, so vacant of a bloody carcass, entrails swarming with flies. *Harvest* moves me to song.

> If I harvest you
> And you harvest me,
> Then we'll go a-roasting together.
> With me-burgers and you-burgers
> And ketchup on top,
> Down the hatch
> And up the chimney,
> Light as birds of a feather.

"Mountain lion hunters took 330 cats, nearly twice the 171 the year before."

Oh, yeah? Where'd the hunters take them to? How many had fresh beef or lamb in their bellies, you suppose? Did the hunters sell the pelts for fur coats or rugs or heads to be mounted on plaques? Nice kitty, sleek kitty.

Put me and a gun in the woods of Idaho, and I'd be one dangerous hunter. Shoot anything that'd move, long as it was on two legs. Blam! Blam!

"Mountain lions took 330 hunters, nearly twice the 171 the year before." Such sinews of steel and lead.

A retired spider

"Retired?" asked Jane. I explained that, as with the spider who came into our bathroom last winter, we had another. He was big, old, and slow moving. On his last legs, you might say. I found him with all eight legs pulled in so he'd present the smallest possible target, or perhaps to keep warm, huddled below the night light in the bathroom. He obviously was keeping his eyes on the light should any moths or other edibles come that way. He'd learned something on his journey through this life. I warned Jane about him so she'd not panic when she saw him.

On another morning I found the old spider in the shower, but noticed him only after I'd turned off the water. He made a show of climbing the wet, slick tiles but got no where. I dangled a tissue at him, and he caught on that. Up he came, crawling slowly over the tissue until I set it down by the mirror, near his night light. At least he carried all his legs he was hatched with.

The retired spider of last year was a sorry sight for spider eyes. He'd lost two of his legs. He moved more slowly. One morning I found him with two more legs gone; someone, perhaps a scorpion, had been nibbling. Lizz made a cruel joke about him walking in circles. I found him one day in a corner of the shower, his life gone, the remaining legs remaining.

Old spiders do die, but they seem to come to our house in the winter on the way.

Where seldom is heard a discouraging word

To think that newspapers should take some responsibility for the content of advertisements is a naive notion. Ads sometimes come in at the last moment. Besides, an editor's job deals with news, not ads; it's not up to the editor to edit ads or to verify statements.

An editor can, though, gently point out to her publisher or ad salesperson that something's fishy about an ad. Or, in this case, something's catty. Or kitty. Or cussedly wrong.

I refer to the tired ad that has been running in our local paper for Hawksnest, that new development on the northeastern slopes of Black Mountain. I know the owners of that pristine property, and I can't blame them for being led astray by their ad-visors or adgencies.

The people who wrote the ad fell into the same trap that snared the developers of Tatum Ranch, causing guffaws from those of us who saw the billboards with the cute little quail. The message: Come live in Tatum Ranch with all this wildlife.

What was funny about that billboard—sickeningly funny—is that the developers had scraped off all the Sonoran desert, driving those quail and their likes away.

What bothers me about the Hawksnest ad is that it refers to a bobcat.

We've seen the bobcat lately on our land. He comes out in the daylight, perhaps because he's disturbed by the bulldozers and trenchers and backhoes working up on Black Mountain. He twitches his tail and acts flustered, as if he'd been driven out by something.

My advice to prospective homesite buyers is to ask to see the bobcat mentioned in the ad. If the Hawksnest hawkers can't produce at least one live individual—not one mounted and hung over a fireplace—then ask about the discount for not providing what the ad promised.

Mountain lions (also called pumas, cougars, and panthers) roam the upper reaches of Black Mountain. The Hawksnest ad doesn't mention them, perhaps because such lions, under stress, have been known in

Colorado to attack such helpless things as dogs, cats, and even grandchildren. Wouldn't do to include a big, bad mountain lion in an ad unless you were trying to reach big-game hunters.

Likewise, Terravita's latest ad carries this laughable headline: "Announcing a grand opening that will last forever." What is Del Webb selling south of Black Mountain, mausoleums? The Sonoran desert, that took 10,000 years to blossom to its present condition, won't last much longer at all with the likes of Terravita, also called Terrauppa and Terrorvita. Reminds me of those wise used car ads that say, "Won't last long." If it won't last, why would you want to buy it?

But an editor can't be responsible for ads, anyway. It's enough to try to keep lies out of the editorial.

What the hell can an antelope say?

That blind squirrel

A mouthful squirrel

I hate him because he has tunneled under the office, excavating a ton of rotting granite that makes the west side look like a mining operation. Yet I love him for his similarities to me. He's getting old.

I watched him from six inches away today, through a pane of glass below the bird feeder. He nibbled along the window ledge, stuffing cheeks with what the finches and cardinals and thrashers and gila woodpeckers dropped. He never flinched when I poked my face in his because, I guess, he's nearly blind. The gray squirrel, whose body is no more than ten inches long, apparently picks up fallen seeds by smell and by touch. He surely can't see the little things, because he can't see me through the window, although the birds can. They scatter when I approach. The squirrel goes on stuffing his cheeks until he looks like an advanced case of mumps. The cheeks swell bigger than his testicles.

Yesterday, working on the roof, I threw handfuls of gravel at the squirrel. It irked me that he was getting seed I put out for birds—and that I was feeding this miserable animal that had tunneled my office floor. I'd spot him from the roof, heave a handful of rock, and watch him flee. When he stood still, though, the squirrel almost disappeared into the background, so perfectly colored is his fur. He is not uniformly gray, I notice now from six inches. The fringes of the fur are banded in dark brown or black. Stopped, he becomes almost invisible. My stones do not bother his bones; he returns as soon as I return to my roof work. No matter. Seeing him closeup today, I find a fondness for him, for his ability to get by minus his poor eyesight. He has captured me with his abilities and his inability. He is safe on my land now.

The blind squirrel, again

I came down the steps from the office and saw him heading for me. I froze. Loping carefully, his tail echoing his wavelike moves, he carried a magenta cactus fruit in his mouth. He brushed by my shoe, hesitated a moment as if smelling something foreign, then continued up the steps to his burrow under my office. I could have reached down and touched him with my hand, but the scare might have given him heart failure. He is too precious for that.

Colophon

Printed in the USA by McNaughton & Gunn, Saline, Michigan, on fifty-pound JB Offset. Cover color separations scanned by Parkwest Graphics, Scottsdale, Arizona. Book designed in Ventura Professional Publisher version 2.0 on a generic personal computer using an Intel 80486 microprocessor running at 33 megaHertz. Output on an LX-29000 TrueImage laser printer from the Printer Works at 300 dots per inch. Text is 12/14 ITC Bookman light with ITC Bookman demi italic headlines. Production by Carefree Communications, Carefree, Arizona.